Charlyne,

Hope you enjoy the book!

Best Wishes for 2016 —

Martha B. Owens

P.S. Lamar sends his love ♡

CHARLIE'S LAST Wish

MARTHA B. OWENS

WESTBOW
PRESS®
A DIVISION OF THOMAS NELSON
& ZONDERVAN

Scripture taken from the King James Version of the Bible.

WestBow Press books may be ordered through booksellers or by contacting:

WestBow Press
A Division of Thomas Nelson & Zondervan
1663 Liberty Drive
Bloomington, IN 47403
www.westbowpress.com
1 (866) 928-1240

ISBN: 978-1-5127-0310-8 (sc)
ISBN: 978-1-5127-0312-2 (hc)
ISBN: 978-1-5127-0311-5 (e)

Library of Congress Control Number: 2015911432

Print information available on the last page.

WestBow Press rev. date: 08/21/2015

Acknowledgments

Thanks to all my friends who continue to believe I have something to share.

Lamar, you have had to put up with me on the computer day and night and fondly tell everyone you are a computer widower. Thank you for not complaining, except when the toilet needs cleaning! You are a wonderful cook and husband. How could I ask for more?

Loraina, Connie, Kathy, Ethel, and Linda, I am so glad you are a part of my life. I love you and appreciate all your input in helping me with ideas, and I thank you for believing in me. What would I do without you? You were my ears when I needed them, which was often. Thank you all for listening and laughing with me when we all needed an outlet. You fill my life with laughter!

Brother Tom, you were instrumental in helping me to make this book the best it could be grammatically. I am so grateful you took the time to do so!

Also, I would like to thank Happy Acres Ranch Inc. for allowing me to use their name in my book.

Last but not least, I thank the good Lord for giving me the patience to persevere when I wasn't sure I had anything left to give. Without Him, I am nothing.

Dedication

In memory of Charles (Charlie) Richardson, and in honor of his wife, Loraina.

As I began to write this book, I had an idea in mind, but wasn't sure where I was going with it. While I was writing, circumstances happened. After the death of our beloved Charlie, my writing changed to bring his name into the storyline.

Keep in mind this is a book of fiction, but Charlie wasn't. I wanted to keep his memory alive; therefore, I was led to call this Charlie's Last Wish. He was a beloved member of the family who is greatly missed. He was just a simple man after God's own heart and a friend to everyone he met.

In my Father's house are many mansions: if it were not so, I would have told you. I go to prepare a place for you. And if I go and prepare a place for you, I will come again, and receive you unto myself; that where I am, there ye may be also. (John 14: 2–3)

Chapter 1

Cathleen was happy living with her parents in a subdivision right outside of Brooklyn, New York. Theirs was one of the nicer homes in the area of tree-lined streets and friendly neighbors. The newly painted, shuttered frame house had been well cared for over the years. An inviting front porch with a swing was on the west side of the house. She and her mom spent many sunny school-day afternoons on the porch before her mom became sick.

For the most part, it was a quiet neighborhood, although you could occasionally hear dogs bark. The family had a cocker spaniel named Daisy. Cathleen and her family knew almost everyone on the street, where her mom and dad had lived for twenty-one years. Her dad, Daniel, had bought the house when he and her mom moved to the States. He and his wife, Margaret, had come from Ireland because they wanted to be a part of the American dream.

They were newlyweds when Margaret became pregnant with her first child, but she miscarried soon after they arrived. She was told she couldn't have any more children, but two years later, Cathleen was born.

Daniel was able to get a job at the steel mill, which was a booming business at the time. He wasn't afraid of work and was promoted to foreman right away. Cathleen remembered him coming home from work when she was small. He entered the house asking, "Where are my girls?" Cathleen always ran up to him, and he picked her up in his dirty work clothes and placed his hard hat on her head. That riled up her mom, and she would say, "Oh, Danny, couldn't you wait until you cleaned up?"

Cathleen and her father would look at each other with mischievous grins, and Daniel would say, "Next time!" Cathleen carried these good memories in her heart and came to rely on them when the days became too long for her to manage alone. Her memories and faith were all she had now.

Cathleen was only ten when her mom came down with an autoimmune disease that caused muscle spasms, difficulty walking, and depression. It was a big responsibility for a young girl, but she loved being able to help her mom. Daniel was a burly man who took good care of his family until hard times struck last year, when he was laid off from the mill. They barely got by on unemployment and what savings he had managed to put away.

One Friday night on her seventeenth birthday, Cathleen asked if she could spend the night with a friend from school. She had never spent the night away from home before, and if she had known what would happen, she never would have gone. Trying to cut down on the utility bill, Daniel used as little heat and electricity as possible. But it was a cold night, so he lit the kerosene heater in the bedroom. After reading the want ads in the paper, he laid the newspaper in a chair by the bed. In the night, Daisy jumped onto the chair, knocking the paper to the floor. It landed so close to the heater it ignited. Flames spread across the bed before anyone could wake up.

Cathleen did not learn of the fire until the next morning. She had no other family here, so the local church was a godsend. She knew she would never have made it without them. She was so glad her parents were Christians and had so many friends at the Catholic Church they attended.

Cathleen's parents had not talked much about their relatives, but she knew she had grandparents living in Ireland; she just didn't know how to get in touch with them. The firefighters on the scene hadn't been able to salvage much from the fire except for a few pictures and a Bible, which were found unharmed. They were in the living room closet, and the fire hadn't reached them. She now kept them in a small piece of luggage in the closet at the home of her friend Emily, where she was staying for now, along with the few clothes she had left. A small metal box containing some papers was found in another closet. Inside were her birth certificate and other paperwork, which meant nothing to her now. Maybe in time she could sit down and look through them. Right now she had to learn to cope each day without her family.

Cathleen's neighbors were kind, and some of them had offered to let her stay with them but the neighborhood held too many memories, and it would have been too difficult to stay there. She had her friend Emily, the one she had spent that night with, to talk to, but even that was difficult now. The church offered to let her stay in a shelter downtown until she turned eighteen, so she had a year to get her life in order.

She was glad to have her own room there, because she was shy and used to being only with her family when not in school. She didn't want to have to talk about what happened, so she was content to be alone and study. She had always been interested in social studies and was leaning toward becoming a social worker, because she saw firsthand the need for more help in that field. She was hoping for a scholarship to NYU or somewhere nearby. She was a smart girl and would figure out her future in due time. Right now, she was still grieving and trying to make sense of what had happened.

Her parents were devout Christians and believed that with faith in God, all things were possible. Cathleen believed it, too, but was having a hard time with her faith right now. "Why?" Cathleen cried out to God. "They were such good people!" Why couldn't she have stayed home that night? If she had, Daisy would have been in her room where she always slept.

She rarely went out, but it was her birthday and she thought it would be nice to be with her friend, Emily, and do what other kids did—for once. Why would God let this happen to the only family she had? She knew she could not keep blaming herself for the accident, because it would keep her from concentrating on school. Cathleen had to keep her grades up if she was going to college on a scholarship.

Since her parents had left Ireland before she was born, Cathleen had never met any of her relatives. She had only known of her dad going back once. However, he never really talked to her about it. Now she had no one to ask, as almost everything they owned and any information they had about the family in Ireland were gone now.

Chapter 2

After Cathleen moved into the shelter, she got a job at Abe's Sandwich Shop within walking distance of her new residence. She was a senior this year. It was not easy working when her heart was so heavy, but she knew she had to keep herself busy and keep money coming in. Her grief counselor told Cathleen to stay busy with work and school so as not to get depressed. She was fighting taking any medication, so staying busy was her best option. The counselor told her to make more friends at school and in the home where she was staying. Being shy, Cathleen thought that was easier said than done.

Cathleen worked the five-to-nine shift, which didn't leave her much time after school, but it kept her mind busy, even though it took a while to get used to the hours. She clocked in right at 5:00 p.m. and started her routine. Some of the employees were classmates from school. They were a year behind her and had cell phones by now, but her family never thought she needed one, and she couldn't afford one now.

She got along well with her boss, and he knew her situation and didn't want to upset her, so he told the other employees not to mention the fire. Cathleen tried to stay busy with her tasks so she wouldn't have to make conversation.

One of her duties was to keep the sandwich bar filled with all the meats, cheeses, and condiments needed to make a good sandwich. She also had to make sure all the different breads were baked as needed. She had to keep her mind on the job, or she would forget to set the timer. She forgot once and nearly burned the bread before another employee rescued it.

She noticed a boy coming in lately and sitting at one of the tables. He was tall and very good-looking with an athletic build, the kind that made girls swoon. Sometimes he would order a sandwich, and other times he just got a drink and chips. They never spoke, but they glanced at each other a few times when he came in. He nodded, and she gave him a half smile. She saw him at school but wasn't in any of his classes. She knew he was on the basketball team, and the girls all seem to like him, but she never saw him with anyone special. Maybe he was a loner too.

He ordered a sandwich tonight and told her his name was Aiden. It was her job to take it to him. She wanted to be polite, and the counselor had encouraged her to make friends. So she carried the sandwich to him and spoke his name. He looked up from his book and said, "Yes, thank you."

Cathleen asked, "By any chance, are you Irish, since you have an Irish name?"

"Why, yes I am, and who might you be?"

"I'm Cathleen. My parents are from a town in Ireland, not far from Dublin."

"My family lives in a city called Kilkenny, not far from there. Where do you go to school?"

"I go to Abraham Lincoln High."

"What a coincidence. So do I. Why haven't I ever seen you there?"

"I don't know. I've seen you practicing with the basketball team when I pass the gym."

When she had to get back to work, he said, "I'll see you around."

At the end of her shift, he was waiting outside. "Do you live close by?" Aiden asked. Cathleen told him she did. "May I walk you home?" She guessed it would be okay, so she agreed. As they walked the few blocks to the shelter together, they made light conversation, mostly about school, but she did mention she was staying in the Catholic Women's Center for the time being. He told her he would like to know more about her if she didn't mind, so they sat on the steps outside the building she stayed in and talked about their childhood. Cathleen told Aiden how her mom and dad had come to America when they were both eighteen. She told him about her mom getting an autoimmune disease and her dad losing his job. She knew he was wondering why she was in a shelter, but she wasn't ready to tell him about the fire. She didn't want him, or anyone else, feeling sorry for her.

Aiden told Cathleen how he had come to live with an aunt several years ago so he could go to school here and then on to medical school. His parents and a brother were still living in Ireland. He said he wanted to try to get them all here when he became a doctor, but his parents probably would not leave because of their business and their love of Ireland. Like Cathleen, he had a 4.0 GPA. His aunt was a nurse, and his family was able to support him very well. With no financial problems, Aiden was able to spend his spare time playing sports and volunteering at the local food bank. Time seemed to fly by as they sat there talking, and Cathleen realized it was getting late.

"Well, I have to go in now. It was nice talking to you."

"It was a pleasure for me, also," said Aiden.

He watched her go in before he headed toward his aunt's house a few blocks over. He was thinking of what a nice girl she seemed to be, and her striking good looks did not hurt, either. There was sadness about her he couldn't quite put his finger on. He wondered why she was staying in the shelter downtown. Maybe he could meet her parents one day and they could talk about their homeland.

Chapter 3

Aiden had heard news at school about a fire that had destroyed a home, along with the family inside a few weeks ago, but he didn't know it was Cathleen's family. It was strange they had never run into each other at school before, not even at the church they both attended. Cathleen had not been going lately because it was such a sad remembrance of her last visit: her parents' memorial service. She had kept their ashes in the boxes provided by the crematorium. The church had been helping her, but she knew she had to earn her own way. She prayed for the Lord to show her what to do, because she felt she could not go on without some divine intervention.

She took her Bible from the closet and opened it up. As she was reading from the book of First Corinthians, a piece of paper fell out. She picked it up, and written on it was an address from a town near Dublin, Ireland, called Wexford. It was from Charles O'Connor, so Cathleen assumed it was her dad's family. "They probably don't know what happened, so I will have to write and tell them," she said aloud. No one could hear her anyway, and she was used to talking to herself now. She sat down and penned a letter to send off to that address. It read:

> *Dear Sir,*
>
> *I am Cathleen O'Connor, daughter of Daniel and Margaret O'Connor. Six weeks ago, while I was not at home, a fire swept through my parents' home, and they were not able to make it out. I am devastated to tell you the news. I found your name and address in our family Bible, which the firemen were able to save.*
>
> *I don't know if you are my dad's brother or father. Having been born in the United States, I have never met any of my relatives in Ireland. Would you please respond and let me know who you are, and what relatives I have there? I am their only living child. I will be looking for a response.*
>
> *Sincerely,*
> *Cathleen*

She decided to mail the letter on the way to school tomorrow. As she prepared to go to sleep, she knelt down beside her bed and gave thanks for finding the address, and for God watching over her. "I can't do this alone, Lord, so I am asking for your help and guidance." Cathleen felt a sense of relief as she lay down, and she slept more peacefully that night than she had in a long time.

On the way to the bus stop the next day, she passed a mailbox on the corner, but Cathleen realized she had no stamp to put on her letter and didn't know what it would cost. Therefore, she put it in her book bag and made a mental note to go to the post office later. Her plan was to mail it before going to work that evening.

The day passed quickly, and Cathleen stopped by her locker to put away the books she wouldn't need to take with her. She had just enough time to get to the post office before going to work, and when she got there, she opened up her book bag and couldn't find the letter anywhere. She must have put it in her locker by mistake. "Please help me find the letter," she prayed softly. She got to work early, but the shop was so busy that her boss let her clock in. She needed to concentrate on her job now and worry about the letter later.

Aiden stayed after school to practice basketball. He had played as a kid in Kilkenny and had taken it up at age twelve, when he had begun living with his aunt. They went back home every year for a visit, but he was accustomed to American ways now. He was tall and agile, so sports were easy for him. What was not so easy to forget was the maiden at the sandwich shop. She had long blonde hair with red highlights, and her eyes, though sad, were a beautiful bright green. He couldn't believe he had never seen her at school before. He made a promise to himself to try and get her to laugh more often. If she was working tonight, maybe he could walk her back to the shelter again. He still wondered why she was staying there, but he wouldn't feel right asking about it so soon.

Chapter 4

When Cathleen clocked out of work that night and headed home, Aiden was waiting for her. She seemed very preoccupied, and he asked if she wanted to talk. She told him about losing the letter she had written and that she hoped she would find it tomorrow. She still hadn't mentioned her parents' death, thinking it was too soon to tell a near stranger. Maybe he already knew about it from school or church and didn't want to bring it up yet, either. She was just glad to have him for a friend as long as he was willing to be one.

Cathleen told Aiden her parents had never told her much about Ireland, but said she would love to go there one day to meet her relatives. Aiden said he and his aunt tried to visit once a year, and told her how beautiful it was there, and he was sure she would love it too. They didn't tarry with each other tonight, as they both had homework. "See you later," said Aiden as he left for his aunt's house.

Cathleen took an earlier bus to school the next day so she could check her locker for the letter. It was nowhere to be found. She knew she could rewrite it, but she decided to go to the dean's office and asked if anyone had turned in a letter without a stamp on it. The dean smiled and said, "Yes, a letter was found by one of the janitors working after school, and he recognized your name because he knew about what happened to your parents. He asked if it was okay if he dropped it off at the post office on his way home; I thought it was really kind of him, so I agreed."

"Could you tell me his name, so I can personally thank him?" The dean wrote his name on a piece of paper and handed it to her. She quickly put it in her pocket and went to class. *What a relief that was*, she thought. *I will look him up later.*

Cathleen didn't have to work that evening, so she hung around the school to wait for the janitor. She walked down to the gym while she was waiting and saw Aiden and several of his teammates shooting hoops. Aiden was in line to shoot next when he looked up and saw Cathleen standing there. For some reason, he got butterflies and missed the hoop. His friends teased him about it but he didn't care. He walked over and asked why she was still at school. She told him about the janitor finding her letter and mailing it for her and that she wanted to thank him. She wasn't working tonight, she said, so she had some spare time.

"If you wait around awhile, I'll ride the bus home with you."

"Okay. I'll come back after I find the janitor," she replied.

She spotted Mr. Rodrigues down the hall from her locker, so she hurried that way and called out his name. He turned around, recognized her, and stopped. His daughter Maria was her age, and she was the one who told him about the fire, and pointed her out to him one day. She was in a couple of Cathleen's classes, but Maria had never spoken to her. "Mr. Rodrigues, I'm Cathleen O'Connor. You found the letter to my family in Ireland, and I want to thank you and pay you the postage for mailing it for me."

"That was no problem, miss. I was happy to do it for you, and you owe me nothing. It was a blessing for me."

"Well, thank you, sir, and if you ever get downtown to Abe's Sandwich Shop, I will treat you to one of our great sandwiches." He thanked her but told her it was not necessary.

It was sunny when Aiden's team finished practicing, and he caught up to Cathleen before she could get back to the gym. He had pulled his sweatpants over his shorts, and when they got off the bus, he asked if she would like to go for an ice cream. It was chilly but not enough to stop her from eating her favorite dessert, so she agreed.

The ice cream shop down the street from the shelter was a nice walk, so they could enjoy eating while walking back. They each got their favorite. As they tried to talk and eat, the ice cream started to melt and run down their chins. They had forgotten to get napkins, and Aiden started wiping his mouth on his shirt. Cathleen looked in her bag and pulled out a handkerchief. They both laughed as she tried to wipe her and Aiden's chins off. She was glad she didn't have to work tonight. She had not been able to talk or laugh this much in a long time, and it felt good.

They sat on the steps again, and he finally asked her why she was living in the shelter if her parents lived in the suburbs. She felt she had to tell him now what had happened. Her parents had died two months ago, but it still felt like it had happened yesterday. He felt bad when she started crying. "Please don't cry," he said. "You don't have to talk about it if it makes you sad."

"Yes, I do. My counselor told me not to hold it in, so I need to tell you what happened." As she finished talking, Aiden had a much deeper respect for the lovely, sad-eyed girl he had become infatuated with. He understood now why she seemed so withdrawn at times. He asked if they had a burial site, and she told him she had their ashes and hoped to take them back to Ireland one day. She had her dog Daisy's ashes, too, but said she would keep them with her. Aiden said he wanted to take her to meet his aunt soon. She had no children, and it might be good for them to meet each other.

His heart quickened as he looked at this beautiful girl. He wanted to kiss her, but he didn't, worried that she might think he felt sorry for her, though nothing could have been further from the truth. He admired her strength and perseverance to go on without any family in this country now—and her beauty didn't hurt, either. She had a way of holding herself that would make one think she could be a model if she chose to. But her looks were the farthest thing from her mind right now. Aiden told her good night and asked if he could see her again

"You know where I work," she said, smiling, and went inside.

Chapter 5

Maria watched for Cathleen when she went to her social studies class. She couldn't talk to her now, but when class was over, she went up and introduced herself and said she was glad her dad had found the letter. They struck up a conversation, and Maria told her that her parents were from Mexico and that she understood what it was like to be away from your relatives.

"I have two younger siblings," Maria said, "a brother and a sister. I have to care for them after school sometimes when my mother works late. She is a housekeeper for a prominent family in the city. She's a wonderful cook and makes the best Mexican food!"

"I've never had Mexican food," Cathleen replied.

"Well, you'll have to come over sometime and eat with us," said Maria.

"Thank you for the invitation," said Cathleen, and she headed to her next class. Everyone was being so kind to her. How could she not respond back with kindness? She had just met this family, and now they were inviting her to their home. She wondered if this was God's way of answering her prayers by putting good people in place for her. She must get up Sunday and attend church. She had put off going long enough now.

The March winds had arrived, and new leaves were starting to come back on the trees, and flowers were starting to bloom. It was almost springtime, and Cathleen's mom had always loved this time of year. Cathleen thought about how her mom had gone from being such a vibrant woman to being confined to a wheelchair. She had loved sitting by the window and watching the newness of flowers and trees in bloom. Cathleen would find her sitting there when she came home from school. Her mom had never talked much about living in Ireland, and Cathleen wondered if she ever missed her family there.

Cathleen knew her parent's death had brought them a newness of life in heaven and that her mother was now well again. She thought about how Paul says in Philippians 1:21 *to die is to gain.* She believed that her parents' had gained more in heaven than they ever had here on earth, and she knew she would see them again one day. Cathleen decided that this was the time to try to shed her grief and focus on the positive. Just look how many friends she had gained—and now she would try to find out about her relatives living in Ireland.

Cathleen thought of the metal box the fireman had handed her and went to the closet to look through it. When she looked underneath her birth certificate, there were insurance papers. Apparently her dad had taken out insurance on the house, and to her amazement, he had also had life insurance on him and her mom. She had never thought to look for this, and the values of the policies were staggering for this poor little Irish girl who was trying to make ends meet in a sandwich shop. She didn't know quite what to do with them, so she decided to ask her counselor for help. Cathleen had not seen her for a couple of months now but was sure she would see her if she called.

She was able to get an appointment quickly, and she took the box with her, holding it close as she rode the bus to her counselor's office. Mrs. Warren was happy to see Cathleen and noticed a big change in her demeanor. She almost seemed happy, and the sadness had disappeared from her eyes. Mrs. Warren was pleased when Cathleen told her about working at the sandwich shop and even meeting a nice boy there—clarifying that they were just friends. When Cathleen showed the insurance papers to her, Mrs. Warren was pleasantly surprised by Cathleen's find. She offered to make the necessary phone calls for her and help her fill out the paperwork, so that was a big relief. Maybe Cathleen would be able to quit her job soon and concentrate more on getting her education. Being a senior, she wanted to get into a good college in the fall, so she needed to be checking those out.

In the meantime, Cathleen's thoughts returned to reality— and to work tonight. She clocked in at her usual time, but they were short of help tonight and asked if she could stay until closing, which was 11:00 p.m. She felt she had no choice, as they needed her, so she got busy filling up the condiments and baking bread. The meat had to be sliced, and time flew by quickly. She had never helped close up before, but the manager told her what she needed to do. Right before they had a chance to lock up, a weird-looking man with long hair and a scraggly beard barged through the doors waving a gun and told the manager and another employee to lock the door and get on the floor. His clothes were dirty and ragged, and his eyes were bloodshot. The manager knew what the work handbook said about robberies, so they both complied.

Cathleen had been taking the trash out and had no idea what was happening. She picked up the broom to start sweeping when she heard the noise from the front. She knew something was wrong by her manager's tone, so she peeked through the door. She wasn't sure what to do but knew she had to do something. The manager and the other girl working tonight were lying on the floor. The keys were still in the door, and the robber opened the cash drawer, and removed the money, stuffing the bills in a paper sack he had brought with him. He went to the door to unlock it and leave—and that's when Cathleen sprang into action. She hit the robber with the broom handle and stunned him before knocking him to the floor and straddling him. This gave the manager time to get up and help. He helped Cathleen hold the man down while the other employee called the police.

When the police arrived and handcuffed the robber, it finally sank in what she had just done. She didn't know how she had managed to do that, and now she was trembling. The police asked if she needed to go to the hospital, but she declined. Her manager told her how brave she was to do that but added that her actions were very dangerous and that she could have gotten hurt. The police officer laughed and said, "Not with this gun. It's not real." Nevertheless, the ordeal had still been scary, and it was not going to be forgotten soon.

It was almost midnight before they could all leave, and Cathleen asked if they could call the shelter to let them know what happened. She was not supposed to be out late unless she had a good reason and they knew about it. The police cleared it with the shelter and said they would take her home. Cathleen did not get much sleep that night, but she was grateful they had caught the crook.

She was a hero at work now, and the news made it into the local paper. They let her have the next night off to catch up on much-needed rest. They teased her at work and offered to let her close more often, but she laughed and said no thanks—she would stick to her regular hours.

Aiden had not seen her all day but had heard about the robbery and caught up with her after school. He gave her a high five for the good deed and invited her to his aunt's house for dinner. "Can I take a rain check on that?" she asked. She was still somewhat in shock, and she really needed to stay home tonight. Aiden agreed and promised he would ask again soon.

Chapter 6

Cathleen checked to see if she had received any mail at the shelter she now called home—and she had. One piece of mail was from Ireland, and the other was from the house insurance. In the first letter, she discovered Charles O'Connor happened to be her dad's father, her grandfather. He said he was glad to hear from her. He knew Daniel had spoken of a daughter and was heartbroken to hear the news of their deaths. He said he would love to see her, but he and her grandmother were elderly now and it would be too long a trip for them to come to America. Was there any chance she could come there? He said there were lots of cousins who wanted to meet her and hear all about America. He offered to send the money for the trip, but she did not feel right taking money from people she had never met. Cathleen didn't know how she could possibly afford to go on her income.

When she opened the second letter, it was a check from the house insurance company. Overcome with sadness and joy at the same time, she sat down on the bed. The memory of what had happened was almost too much to bear. She was astonished at the amount, which would make many things possible now. Her counselor had sent off the death certificates, and now they were waiting to hear from their life insurance. Even with the money, she knew she couldn't go to Ireland until school was out anyway, so she decided to write him back. It would be nice to finally meet her relatives.

Cathleen got ready for bed after picking up a sandwich and a piece of fruit from the kitchen. The shelter had scheduled mealtimes, but there were always a few sandwiches and fruit handy for some of the residents. As she lay in bed, she thought of what she had been through the last seven years with her mom's disease. Yes, it had been hard, but she had also been happy. She could not have asked for better parents, and she was glad she was finally going to be able to meet all of her relatives. She couldn't believe she would be financially able to go to Ireland now. Maybe now she could get a cell phone. Aiden had one, so they could exchange numbers.

As she drifted off to sleep, she dreamed of fields of flowers, and the young and old, all dancing around her mom and dad with smiles on their faces.

She was anxious to tell Aiden about hearing from her grandfather and about getting the check that would enable her to visit Ireland. After she told him, he said he was happy for her. He was just getting to know her, and he liked what he knew. He hoped she would not be gone long. They were never able to spend much time together because of her work and his sports practices, but when they did, he felt they were bonding. He liked walking her home, because then they had more time together. He told her he would see her after work.

It had been a month since she'd heard from her grandfather, and she had written him back, giving him her cell number, and telling him how much she looked forward to coming there. Today another letter came, and it was from her aunt Clare, her father's sister. She told Cathleen her grandfather had had a stroke but was doing better now and could hardly wait to meet his granddaughter. She gave Cathleen her phone number, and said to call if she could come. She remembered how fast her parents were gone from her, so she made an appointment with her counselor and explained the circumstances.

Since she had a 4.0 GPA and the school year was almost up, she was sure the dean would give her some time off. She could take some assignments with her and mail them back, if necessary. She was sure she would still be able to graduate, and would start applying to several colleges in the area.

Mrs. Warren said Cathleen would have to get a passport first, and then she would call and get Cathleen a flight out. It was good she had found her birth certificate in the metal box, or there would have been more delays.

She checked in at the sandwich shop at her usual time and started her tasks. When she got a break, she went to the office, explained her situation to the manager, and let him know she would need to take some time off. Her manager was very understanding and told her to take all the time she needed; she would still have a job when she got back.

When she called her aunt Clare and told her when she was coming, she was told someone would be at the airport to pick her up. Aiden borrowed his aunt's car and was able to take her to the airport. He sat with her until the passengers were able to board the plane. When it was time for Cathleen to board the plane, Aiden hugged her and said, "My aunt wants to meet you when you come back, so you have an invitation for dinner waiting on you."

"Okay!" she yelled over the sound of the engines as she boarded the plane.

Chapter 7

After the plane landed, she was not sure who to look for, but eventually she spotted a young woman holding up a sign with her name on it. As she walked up, the girl asked, "Are you my cousin Cathleen from America?"

"Yes," said Cathleen. "May I ask who you are?"

"I am Bridget, your aunt Kerry's daughter. Your dad was my mother's brother. That makes us cousins."

"Oh," said Cathleen. This was all so new to her—she had never met any of her relatives and was feeling like a stranger in a foreign land.

"Oh, don't look so forlorn. You'll get used to us quickly. We're just one big happy family."

They put her luggage in the backseat, and Cathleen noticed the steering wheel on the right side of the car, so she got in on the other side. Bridget quickly sped onto the left side of the road, which Cathleen was not used to, and when Bridget saw her face, she laughed. "You'll be safe with me. I promise."

The road to where her grandparents lived was a long and winding dirt road. Her mom was a Murphy before marrying her dad, and both grandparents lived in the countryside not far apart from each other. The O'Connors were all waiting on the large,

25

screened-in front porch for her when she and Bridget arrived. The family spent a lot of their time there, doing some of their chores, and playing lots of music and singing as well.

Her grandfather Charles was well enough to be up, and he was sitting there with her grandmother Myrna. Sitting there seemed to soothe Charles as he sat in his overalls, reminiscing over his younger days when he would sit with the family and play the banjo and sing along.

As Bridget approached the porch, she introduced Cathleen to the family, and her grandmother got up and hugged Cathleen.

"It's so good to finally meet you," Grandmother Myrna said. "Charles, here is your granddaughter, Cathleen."

"Yes, I know who she is," her grandfather said. "She looks like her mother. Please sit down, child."

Cathleen sat down in one of the rockers. It was rather awkward sitting there, not really knowing anything about her relatives. Charles asked about New York and how she liked living there.

"New York is the only place I have lived," she replied.

The more they talked, the more comfortable she became with him. He reminded her of her dad. She told him of her plans to go to college and her hopes of being a social worker.

Seeing that Charles was getting tired, his wife encouraged him to go rest for a while before it was time to eat, and they went inside. They would talk more at the supper table when everyone was there.

Cathleen followed her grandmother up to the second floor to the room where she'd be staying. As she pulled the curtain back, it was like looking into her dream, but without her parents and the other people. There were beautiful fields of flowers everywhere she looked. It was so peaceful here in the countryside—none of the noise from cars and trains she had gotten so accustomed to in New York. But she was not expecting to be here long enough to get used to this.

She opened her suitcase and got out another dress to wear to supper. After a relaxing shower, she dried her naturally curly hair—hair she sometimes thought a curse. Then she went down to meet the rest of the family who lived there.

There were twelve chairs around the table; her grandfather Charles O'Connor was at the head, with her grandmother Myrna next to him. There were so many names to remember—David, Dylan, and Donald, the triplets, with their mother, Cara, and Redmond, her husband. Aunt Clare was there with her husband Dillon. Bridget was there, but her mother, Kerry, was at work. She had been a widow since Bridget was very young, and her husband's family, who lived in Scotland, had lost touch over the years.

Cathleen's grandparents on her mother's side had been invited but had not shown up. She hoped to meet them before she went back.

It was a nice meal with lamb chops, which Cathleen had never eaten, and lots of fruits and vegetables from the garden. Conversation at the table was difficult with the noise from the triplets and their mother shouting at them to behave. They had just turned twelve, and three were more than a handful!

Cathleen offered to help clear the table, but her grandmother said they had plenty of help. The triplets went outside to the porch so the adults could talk; then they would have dessert and tea in the sitting room.

The family asked a lot questions, and she had to repeat the sad story of the fire all over again. They wanted to know how she was doing in school, what she would do afterward, and did she need money? She tried to tell them everything they wanted to know, but not a bit more. She was still getting used to having another family. She told them her parents had left her money so she was okay. She was not sure what she would do with her life but would figure it out along the way. When they finally left her alone, she went by her grandfather's room and asked to sit with him awhile before going to bed. Her grandmother left them alone and said she would be back in soon.

Cathleen felt so comfortable talking to her grandfather that she asked, "May I call you Grandfather Charlie? That's an endearing way of saying your name in America."

He patted her hand and said, "Aye, Colleen, you may call me whatever feels comfortable for you."

"My name is Cathleen, not Colleen."

"I know that, child. *Colleen* is just an Irish term, but I will call you Cathleen if you wish me to."

"It's okay, grandfather. I'm just not familiar with that term."

While they sat together, her grandfather propped himself up on pillows, leaned over, and said, "There's something important I need to tell you."

"What's that, Grandfather Charlie?"

"Your mother was not your real mother. I'm not supposed to tell you, but you need to know. Please find her."

Cathleen was shocked to hear this and asked, "So who is my real mother?"

He started to say her name but stopped himself and said, "Please find her. I want you to get to know your mother and for you both to be happy. Will you promise me you will do that?" Cathleen, not knowing what else to say, said, "Yes, Grandfather Charlie, I will do my best."

Her grandfather asked her to go over to his dresser and open the top drawer. She did as he asked and found a small box lying there. He told her to open it. "This was your great-grandmother's. It's a claddagh ring, and I want you to have it."

"It's beautiful, grandfather! Are you sure you want me to have this?"

"Yes, Colleen, I do." He kissed her on the cheek. "I must rest now," he said, lying back down, promising to visit more with her tomorrow.

Cathleen tucked the box in her pocket and went to her bedroom. She sat down on the bed, stunned by the information she had just received. It was almost too much to take in after losing her parents. She couldn't say anything to her grandmother since she wasn't supposed to know, but she wasn't sure what to do about it now. Maybe she would find out from her mother's side of the family. But wait! Didn't her grandfather just tell her that her mother was not her real mother? Maybe the stroke had affected him and his memory wasn't good. She didn't know whom she could ask—she didn't know these people well enough to confide in them. She wished Aiden were with her. He was so sensible and would know what she should do. Maybe she would be enlightened when she went to visit the other side of the family in a few days.

The next morning, everyone met at the breakfast table. Charles felt like a burden had been lifted from him last night, and he was eager to know his granddaughter better. He asked her if she would ride around the ranch with him, and she said she would be delighted. Her grandmother didn't think he should be out riding so soon, but Grandfather Charlie told her to leave him be. He knew what he could and could not do. He told Cathleen to meet him on the porch in an hour. She changed into a pair of jeans, the only thing she had that was presentable for riding, and waited on the porch for her grandfather.

What a beautiful granddaughter I have, he thought as he drove them down to the barn, where an attendant was waiting, having gotten the word to have two horses ready to ride.

As they rode through the countryside, Cathleen knew this man was in his right mind. She had never ridden a horse before, but she felt comfortable riding with her grandfather, and it was fun riding through the countryside with him. It still felt strange to Cathleen to be here without her parents—she was saddened by the fact that she would never have the chance to experience this with them. There was such a feeling of freedom riding out here with nature. She listened to the love in her grandfather's voice as he described how he had built this land up to where it was today. Cathleen was amazed at all the land he showed her. He used only a small portion for a garden now, but it was big enough to feed their large family and anyone else who needed food. Listening to him, Cathleen got the impression her grandfather had been a prosperous and well-liked man, and she could see why. He had been a hard worker, and she saw where her dad had gotten his work ethic. She doubted her dad had told his father of the hard times he had after losing his job. She saw where she had inherited some of her stubbornness from too.

As they headed back to the barn, she thanked her grandfather for the ride. Neither mentioned what he had told her the night before. She hoped she could get some answers before she headed back to the States. Later, when she asked if someone could drive her over to visit her mother's family, there were curious glances passed around the room before Bridget finally spoke up and said, "I will, Cousin Cathleen, so let's go!"

Chapter 8

As Bridget took her farther up the countryside, Cathleen admired the rolling hills, the wildflowers growing everywhere, and the sheep and cattle nibbling on clover as they whizzed by. Bridget's foot was heavy on the pedal, and Cathleen had to ask her to slow down a couple of times so she could admire the scenery. The flowers were all in bloom, and she rolled her window down so she could smell them. They pulled up to a nice, cottage-style house.

"Just so you know, the Murphys and the O'Connors don't get along real well," said Bridget.

"Why?" asked Cathleen.

"I don't know the whole story because I was a kid when rumors were flying around. I don't know exactly what happened."

"Grandfather Charlie said my mother wasn't my real mother. Do you know what he meant by that?"

"Well, why don't you ask the people who should know?" Bridget said. "We know Uncle Daniel was your dad, so we're still related, no matter what. Do you want me to wait for you?"

"Surely I can get one of them to bring me back, but if I can't, may I call you?"

"Sure," said Bridget, and she wrote her cell phone number down on the back of a receipt.

"Thanks for the ride, Bridget. You can come to visit me in New York someday if you would like."

"I might take you up on that," she said before speeding away, leaving a trail of dust behind her.

A young girl had been watching them through the screen door.

"Hello," said Cathleen. "Are the Murphys at home?"

The girl opened the door and let Cathleen in. "I'm Cathleen O'Connor. What's your name?"

"I'm Kaitlin. My folks are on the back porch. Follow me."

As she entered the house, Cathleen heard music. The song wasn't familiar to her, but it had a nice sound to it. Someone was playing a fiddle, and another a banjo. When they saw her, they stopped playing.

"Hello," she said, "I'm Margaret O'Connor's daughter, Cathleen. I came to visit my grandfather Charlie when I heard about his stroke."

"We know who you are," the older woman spoke up.

"Sorry about your grandfather," one of the men said. "How is he doing?"

He's doing better now, thank you." Cathleen looked at the older couple on the porch and asked, "Are you my mother's parents?"

"Yes," the woman said. "I'm Deidre. "Margaret was my daughter, and Quinlan here was her father. We had to hear about what happened from the O'Connors."

"I would have written to you, but I didn't have your address or phone number."

"What's done is done now, so we have to move on. What do you want from us?" she asked.

"Now, mam, don't be rude," said her grandpa Quinlan. "She probably just wants to meet us."

"Well, why did it take you so long?" asked her grandmother.

Almost in tears at their reception, Cathleen made her answer straightforward. "I couldn't come, because I did not have the money."

"So your other grandparents paid the way?"

"No, I was able to pay my own way with the insurance money from the house fire," she said.

They kept firing questions at her until Cathleen couldn't bear to answer any more and was glad she had brought her cell phone with her. Thank goodness she had gotten Bridget's phone number. When she answered right away, Cathleen told her to pick her up; she would be walking down the road, because she couldn't stay here another minute!

She saw the dust before she saw the car, how grateful that Bridget drove fast.

"Why didn't you warn me?" asked Cathleen once she was in the car.

Bridget smiled and said, "I tried to."

"My mother wasn't like them at all. She was sweet and kind."

"Well, all I can say is not all family members are the same. Look at my crazy family—and then there's *crazy*! You just met up with the latter."

"I need to know who my real mother is," Cathleen begged.

"Better yet, I'll take you to see her if you will stay longer." Cathleen agreed so that she could find her mother, and hopefully get some questions answered by Bridget.

"Now where do we go?" Cathleen asked.

"You'll see in a few minutes" was Bridget's reply.

They turned onto a road lined with big, beautiful red maple trees and came upon a facility that looked like a nursing home but was surrounded by a wall with a security gate. Bridget showed her license to the gatekeeper and told them they were going to see Darcy Murphy.

"Is this one of my cousins?" Cathleen asked, and Bridget said, "You'll see."

They parked outside and went onto a large porch with rocking chairs used by the residents and employees. Bridget did the talking as they entered through the front doors and walked to the desk to get a pass to go to Darcy's room. Cathleen noticed that there was even security for the halls. *What have I gotten myself into?* she wondered. When they entered Darcy's room, she was strapped to a wheelchair.

"Why is she tied up?" Cathleen asked.

"So she doesn't fall out," said Bridget.

Darcy looked up in surprise to see who had come through the door. Was she dreaming again? She had dreamed of her fair-haired daughter for so long now; she must be hallucinating from the drugs they gave her.

Cathleen looked at Darcy and was reminded of her mother, though Darcy was a few years younger.

"This is Darcy, your birth mother," Bridget said.

Cathleen gasped at her words, but could certainly see the resemblance. Both Darcy and her mother, Margaret, had the same golden hair and green eyes. Darcy recognized her daughter right away, and tears came spilling down her cheeks. Cathleen found a tissue and wiped her tears and her mother's away.

"Why was this kept such a secret?" Cathleen asked.

"I'll try to explain what I know on the way home, okay?" Bridget said. "Just enjoy your mom for now."

Darcy asked about Margaret and Daniel, and Cathleen didn't know what to say. Apparently, no one had told her. Cathleen looked at Bridget, and Bridget said, "They are both fine. Cathleen wanted to come and see you." They both cried and held hands. Darcy said, "I knew you would find me one day."

Mother and daughter had little to say to one another. Cathleen didn't really know much about her yet, and Darcy's condition made it hard for her to rationalize what was happening. As Cathleen and Bridget prepared to leave, they both said, "I love you," and Cathleen promised to come back before she left Ireland.

As they pulled upon the highway, Bridget said, "Okay, this is what I heard over the years. After your mom and dad moved to America, your mom had a miscarriage. Darcy went over to help Margaret while Daniel worked. After hearing she couldn't have any more children, Margaret went into a deep depression for a while, and shut Daniel out of her life. Well, one thing led to another, and Darcy became pregnant with Daniel's baby.

Darcy agreed to stay and have the baby, and give her to them before she flew home. She gave her name on the birth certificate as Margaret O'Connor. The baby was enough to bring Margaret out of her depression, and Darcy promised never to try and see her, or let her know. The knowledge of what she had done finally took a toll on her, and she attempted suicide a few months ago."

Cathleen sat silent as Bridget told the story as she knew it. She wondered if there were other secrets in this family she didn't know about. She told Bridget she couldn't understand how this could split a family up because she was still their granddaughter, no matter what happened.

Bridget then told her about the land that both families had wanted. There were several acres of land between their property, and the O'Connors ended up buying it before the Murphys, and there had been a rift between them long before their children married.

Well, at least that made a little more sense to Cathleen, but not enough to harbor a grudge for this long.

Chapter 9

Cathleen was physically and mentally exhausted when she arrived back at her grandfather Charlie's house. The nightly meal had already been served, but Bridget and Cathleen were able to eat ham sandwiches and leftover salad before they headed for bed. Cathleen prayed for both families that night—that they would lay their anger aside and forgive and forget. Didn't they get a granddaughter from the mistake Daniel and Darcy made? Otherwise, there would never have been a Cathleen. Since she wouldn't be leaving for a few days, she would be able to visit with her mother again before returning to the States.

The next day, there wasn't much conversation at the O'Connors about where the two had been the day before, but everyone put two and two together and could tell Cathleen knew who her real mother was now. Of course, they couldn't blame their son, Daniel, so it must have been Darcy's fault. Cathleen hoped to get to know her family better. It had been too long already, and she needed a relationship with the only family she had left.

Cathleen got a ride back to her other grandparents' home and told them she was sorry things had turned out the way they did and suggested that they stay in touch now. She left the address and her cell phone number, along with the number at the shelter and told them she would let them know when she got a new address. She hugged them all and told them she loved them and would visit again. The Murphys seemed more compassionate than last time and wished her well.

Before Cathleen left the next day for the airport, she asked the O'Connors if she could pray with them. Grandfather Charlie led the prayer, then Cathleen ended the prayer by asking that both families would unite, and not harbor any more grudges against each other. Then she asked the angels to watch over the plane that was taking her home.

They all hugged, and Bridget threw Cathleen's luggage in the car and said, "Let's go, cuz, time's a-wasting." She sure didn't have to worry about being late with Bridget behind the wheel!

On the way to the airport, Bridget took Cathleen by to see her mom. Darcy looked better today, and she had gotten dressed for her daughter's return. Darcy was more cognizant, and as they talked, Cathleen told her about her aspirations of being an advocate for families one day. Before leaving, they hugged, and Cathleen promised to come back as soon as she could. Cathleen called Aiden and left a message that she was on her way home, but didn't leave any more information. Bridget waited at the airport until Cathleen boarded the plane, and they both said, "See you soon!"

It was a good feeling when those wheels landed on the tarmac on American soil. She had not communicated with Aiden since she left him a message, and hated to bother him, so she expected to take a cab back to her residence. However, like a trooper—and the smart guy he was—Aiden had been checking the flights coming in from Ireland every day and found out which flight she would be on. He wanted to surprise her, so he borrowed his aunt's car, and they were both a welcome sight to Cathleen.

Before he knew what he was doing, he picked her up, twirled her around, and kissed her! It took them both by surprise, and he apologized for his behavior. She said she understood because she had missed him too. He asked if she could come to his aunt's house and have a good meal. Then they could talk all they wanted. She didn't have a reason to go back to the shelter except to drop her luggage off and freshen up. Aiden said he would wait for her in the car.

They talked as Aiden drove her to his aunt Fiona's house. Aiden told Cathleen about what it was like growing up in Kilkenny. He had one older brother, Kevin, who worked with his dad, who was once a plant manager at a gas company, but his dad had eventually opened his own business. Aiden said he had relatives that fished for a living, some who worked in the mines, and an uncle who owned a pub in Dublin. Besides his aunt, Aiden had been the only one to go to college.

As they entered the small, brick, two-bedroom house, Cathleen could smell the Irish stew cooking. It smelled wonderful! Fiona was stirring the stew as Aiden called out to her that he was home and had brought a guest. "Come into the kitchen," Fiona called back. She removed her apron and came over to Cathleen, shaking her hand.

"Aiden has told me a lot about you. Please make yourself comfortable in my home. Aiden has been a lot of help to me while staying here. I'm glad you two are friends—and that even though you are American born, you still have the Irish blood in you."

"Thank you," said Cathleen. "What's in your stew? It smells delicious!"

"I didn't know if you liked lamb, so I used beef with lots of vegetables and herbs you will recognize when you eat it. I added a little Irish beer, but the alcohol will cook out. I also made homemade soda bread and an apple crumble for dessert."

"Thank you so much for inviting me—well, Aiden invited me, but I know you gave him permission to do so," Cathleen said.

"Yes, of course I did. We have friends, but not a lot of Irish ones."

They sat in the small living room and talked while the stew finished cooking. Fiona told some funny stories about her job at the hospital, and they laughed at her sense of humor.

Aiden had already told his aunt what had happened to Cathleen's parents, so the subject was not brought up. Fiona did ask about her trip back to Ireland, and Cathleen told her how beautiful the countryside was and that she got to meet both sides of her family, though she did not go into details. She wasn't quite sure what she should tell Aiden, so she decided not to say anything yet.

She thanked his aunt for the wonderful meal, and Fiona said Cathleen was invited to come back anytime. She might not get as good a meal as she did tonight, Fiona said, but there was always something on the stove. Cathleen thanked her again for the invite as they left, and Aiden drove her home. It had been a long day, so they said good night on the steps. Aiden hugged her again and gave her a kiss on the cheek. He didn't want to cross any boundaries she wasn't comfortable with, but he was sure tempted.

Chapter 10

Cathleen tossed and turned that night as she recalled everything that had happened in a week's time. She thought her life had been turned upside down before her trip to Ireland. Now that she had all this new information, she felt like her life was in a whirlwind, and she was in the center of it. As she finally drifted off to sleep in the wee hours of the morning, she had the dream again of the field of flowers, with everyone dancing around someone who looked like her—only it wasn't her, but her biological mother, Darcy. She wasn't in a wheelchair anymore, and she looked normal. She remembered it was a happy dream when she woke up. She felt it was the Lord's way of giving her some peace.

Cathleen was back in school. She had only missed a week and had made up the required assignments, so she would be graduating with her class. She was also back at the sandwich shop, and Aiden was always there to walk her home. She told Aiden she needed to start going back to church again and asked if he would come too. He told her he had been going and even stopped by to say a prayer for her when he could. She was touched by that and told him she had more to tell him, but it had to be when she felt the time was right. He said he understood and would not ask.

When two weeks had passed since her trip to Ireland, she found a letter in her mailbox from her cousin Bridget, who would rather write than call, and two checks from her parents' life insurance. It was overwhelming again to see so much money, but she would put them in the metal box where she kept her important papers until she could get to the bank. Then, she opened the letter from her cousin:

> *Dear Cathleen,*
>
> *I hope you are well and over the shock of meeting all your relatives! I think your visit made a difference, because the Murphys have stopped by, and everyone has tried to be cordial. I heard they have been going to visit your mom, Darcy, more often. The rehabilitation center said that she has improved so much since you came to see her and that she will be released soon. I still want to come and visit you there in New York, where all the rich and famous live!*
>
> *Love,*
>
> *Your cousin Bridget*

Cathleen folded the letter up and put it in her box. She was straightening up the contents when she noticed a letter beneath all the paperwork, addressed to her dad. It was from Darcy. It read:

> *My dearest Daniel,*
>
> *My heart is heavy as I write this letter. I am so ashamed of what I let happen between us, and I pray that God will forgive us both for the wrong we did to Margaret. A beautiful*

daughter came from our sin, and I hope she never learns the truth, for it would break Margaret's heart. I probably will never get to see her, but that's my one and only desire before I die. Please tell Margaret to forgive me, and please don't be mad at me. Take good care of your angels, and prayerfully, we will all reunite one day.

With affection,
Darcy

Poor Darcy—she just could not live with her guilt and shame, and she had already convinced herself that she had the same autoimmune disease as her sister. Cathleen was sure Darcy was contemplating suicide when the letter was written but had held onto life as long as she could bear. Didn't she know that she had become a child of God when she accepted Jesus, His Son? She could be forgiven when He shed His blood on the cross. Cathleen was glad it wasn't Darcy's time to go and that God had spared her life so she could make peace with herself—and that Cathleen had finally met her birth mother, as Grandfather Charlie had wished. She had yet to tell her grandfather, but she would find a way to tell him.

Cathleen closed the box and reminded herself to take the checks to the bank tomorrow after school. She would have to start a savings account now that she had more money than she would need for a while. Four months ago, she had lost her parents, didn't have any money or a place to live, and had had to find a job. Now she had learned that her real mother was alive, and she had more money than ever and a real family and friends who cared about her. God hadn't just opened a window—He had opened a door!

Chapter 11

Cathleen had managed to keep her grades up while in Ireland, thanks to her counselor giving her makeup assignments. She would soon be graduating and had decided to keep her job until then. She found out she had been accepted at NYU on a scholarship, but she would still need money for other things.

She was going back to church, and she sat with Aiden and his aunt whenever possible. It was a large church, and she had never realized how many of her friends and teachers went there. She had been so preoccupied with her mother's health that she never paid attention. Mr. Rodrigues and his family attended too. His wife invited her to lunch after church, and since Cathleen thought it would be rude to turn them down, she accepted. She told Aiden she would see him later.

She rode with the family back to their home in the suburbs. They lived on a nice, quiet street, but maybe it was quiet because it was Sunday. It was a Spanish-style house, perfect for this Mexican family. The yard was well kept with a few hedges around the house. There was a tree in the front yard that she thought was an evergreen, with flowers in bloom all around it. She was welcomed in and took her shoes off like the rest of the family. Mrs. Rodrigues worked as a housekeeper and tried to keep her own home as clean as possible.

Maria had set the table already, adding an extra plate in hopes that Cathleen could come. Maria and Cathleen waited in the living room until lunch was ready. They were having a special Mexican meal for Cathleen since she had never had one. Lupe Rodrigues had gone out of her way to give Cathleen a little taste of everything. This way they could have leftovers all week! What a feast it was, too, with taquitos and enchiladas on homemade tortillas, tamales, refried beans, and rice. They had cookies called *galletas* in Spanish. Mr. Rodrigues said grace in Spanish and then again in English so Cathleen could understand. Cathleen was full after the meal and asked if she could take a couple of the galletas home.

After the meal, Cathleen helped clean up, as was her custom, and they all sat down together, except the little ones, who scampered outside. Cathleen wanted to know how they had come to live in New York, and Mr. Rodrigues—Juan—told her of his brother, José, who had come over first. He got a job with the school system after he arrived and sent for his brother. Juan was able to work with Jose' until he was transferred to Abraham Lincoln High School. He and his wife became citizens, and their children were born here. He told Cathleen how his ancestors had made their money by making things with their hands. They were very talented and made pottery, jewelry, hand-crafted rugs, quilts, and shoes they called *Zapatas.*

Cathleen didn't have a lot to share, but she told them about her visit to Ireland. She explained that she had made the trip because of her grandfather's illness. She talked about how her cousin had sped up and down the winding roads through the countryside on the wrong side of the road. Everyone laughed as she talked about her cousin being a little on the wild side for her. She said the countryside was beautiful, the food was wonderful, and she loved seeing the wildflowers growing everywhere.

When it was time for her to go home, Mr. Rodrigues and Maria drove her back to the shelter. As Cathleen got out of the car, she invited Maria to come over sometime, and Maria said she would. Sitting outside on the steps was Aiden.

"How long have you been waiting?" she asked.

"Not long. I gave you a couple of hours there and thirty minutes to get back."

It was amazing the way he could figure things out when it came to her. She sat down on the step beside him and told him how nice the Rodrigues family was. She told him about the fantastic Mexican meal she had just had. She shared one of the cookies with him, and she knew it was good by the way he inhaled it. They sat there and made light conversation until neither had much to say. Aiden wanted to tell Cathleen how much he liked her but didn't want to scare her off. He had never seen her with anyone, so he was content to let things be the way they were for now.

Chapter 12

Graduation was around the corner, and everyone was having their pictures taken and getting fitted for their gowns. Maria was graduating also, so her family would be there. It was sad for Cathleen that her parents had not lived to see her graduate, but she knew they would have been happy for her.

Bridget had called to ask when graduation was, and Cathleen let her know. It had been raining a lot lately, and she was hoping for a beautiful day so they could have it outside. Her manager from the sandwich shop said he would be there, and of course, Aiden's aunt would attend. It would be nice if some of Aiden's family could come, but they said their schedule was too tight right now. She would like to meet them, because she knew he had to have come from a good family. But look at her parents' family—her mom and dad's family used to be like the Hatfields and McCoys, but at least now they seemed to be getting along better, thanks to Grandfather Charlie. She was sure he had been praying for peace between the two families.

She was really starting to like Aiden more as she came to know him, but she knew they couldn't get too serious right now. Education came first. She was hoping to start college in the fall, but her birth mother and grandparents were her priority at the moment. She was able to give her two weeks' notice at work, and on her last day, everyone was acting secretive. Before closing time, all the employees who were off that day showed up and surprised her with a graduation party. She had known something was up when they wouldn't let her go in the cooler and offered to go for her. They brought out the cake and presents and congratulated her on getting into NYU.

On the night of her graduation, she was a little nervous. She was leaving behind all she had ever known and was now moving forward to a new life. She had been looking at apartments and had seen a few she liked a lot. She still had her room at the shelter until she turned eighteen. It was just nice to know what was available so she could fit it into her budget. She knew she was financially well off now, but she wanted to be frugal. For now, she had to shut all of this out of her mind and concentrate on graduating.

Aiden and his aunt would be picking her up anytime now. She sat by the window to watch so they wouldn't have to wait for her. It wasn't long before Fiona's grey sedan pulled up in front, and she locked her door and went out.

It was a packed house, and everyone was lined up to go on stage and receive their diploma indoors. It had rained the night before, so the field was still wet. Cathleen was antsy waiting for the ceremony to start. She looked out into the audience and thought she saw her cousin Bridget and Darcy in the auditorium, but she knew she must be wrong. Bridget never said they were coming, and she was sure they would have let her know if they were.

She put her thoughts aside and concentrated on not falling in her heels. She wasn't used to heels and they hurt her feet, so she kept slipping them off. The principal would call her name about halfway through the service. The line was moving faster than she thought, and she had just managed to get them back on before he called her name. As she walked onto the stage, she heard "Woohoo, Cathleen, way to go!" and looked out into the audience at two women standing up and waving their arms and yelling. It was her cousin and her biological mother! The audience broke out laughing, and all Cathleen could do was smile at her crazy family, get off the stage as quickly as possible without falling down, and sit down.

They found each other when it was over, and Cathleen said, "Why in the world didn't you tell me you were coming? I was beginning to think I was crazy too when I saw you."

"We wanted to surprise you, that's why!" Bridget said. They all hugged and Bridget said, "Let's go to our hotel room and catch up on all the news."

"Where is it?"

"Right around the corner from where you stay. We wanted to be close to you."

"My friend Aiden graduated too, and his aunt is here, so I'll see if we can get a ride back with them so you don't have to take a taxi."

She caught up with Aiden and his aunt and asked for a ride, and all three rode back with them. Bridget invited Aiden and Fiona to the hotel so they could all get acquainted with each other. Fiona said she had to work early in the morning but said that Aiden could stay if he wanted to and walk home later.

Cathleen had never gotten around to telling Aiden the story about who her real mother was, so this was going to be rather complicated for her to try and explain at this moment. She would have to tell Bridget and Darcy to go along with her until she could tell Aiden. Fortunately, he had to excuse himself to the bathroom, and Cathleen had a chance to tell them not to let the cat out of the bag yet!

Bridget was not one to hold back. "You must be real sweet on this guy, and I can see why!" Bridget informed Cathleen that she had told Darcy about the fire before they came to the States. Darcy had been asking about Margaret and Daniel, and Bridget had thought it was time she knew. She had really taken it hard but understood it was a tragic accident.

When Aiden came back, Cathleen introduced Bridget as her cousin, on her daddy's side, and Darcy was her aunt, on her mother's side. Darcy was quiet and shy like her daughter, so she didn't have much to say. Bridget and Aiden did most of the talking. He told them about growing up in Ireland and how his aunt had come to New York several years ago and gone to college to become a nurse. His parents allowed him to come live with her when he was twelve. Since he was young when he came, he said, he had adapted well, and his aunt had put him in sports to keep him out of trouble after school.

Bridget said she was the youngest, and somewhat spoiled by her grandfather. She had dropped out of college after a year and decided she wanted to be a beautician, so she went to cosmetology school. She never worked regular hours but had special clients who paid well when they came to her house. She said her father had died when she was young, and her grandfather helped take care of her and her mom financially, so she wasn't worried about money.

Bridget was fun to be around, and they couldn't help but laugh at some of her escapades.

Aiden asked Darcy what she did for a living, and she said she was in between jobs. She told him she had gone to school to be a social worker but had gotten sick and hadn't finished her education. Cathleen was taken by surprise when she heard that and realized again that she didn't know that much about her birth mother. That must be where she got her love of working with families.

They ordered a pizza, and Aiden and Bridget fought over the last piece but settled on sharing it. It was almost midnight when Aiden walked Cathleen home. They were both happy to be out of school and on to the next chapter of their lives. They talked about what a fun time they had had tonight, and they hugged at her door. Tomorrow would be a new beginning for both of them.

Chapter 13

Bridget and Darcy were able to stay all week and wanted to see everything they could. They took the tour bus to Washington, D.C., and took in all the sights there. They stayed to watch the changing of the guards at the Tomb of the Unknown Soldier. The next day, Bridget wanted to go shopping at all the fancy stores in New York City. Darcy was tired and not that interested in shopping but went because she wanted to be with her daughter. They all bought dresses with fancy shoes and bags to match. That set them back a pretty penny, and their lunch was almost as much.

They decided to stay in that evening and play cards, and Cathleen asked if she could invite Aiden and his aunt. Fiona didn't have to work the late shift, so they were both able to come, and they brought food from one of the local delis with them. Aiden's aunt was a lot of fun when you got to know her, and they played until sore loser Bridget lost—then she was ready to quit. She said she was better at cutting hair than playing cards, and since she just happened to have her scissors with her, they each got a haircut!

Before Bridget and Darcy left for Ireland, the three of them promised not to stay away so long again; they would take turns visiting each other. Aunt Fiona loaned her car to Aiden, and he took them to the airport. They hugged each other, and Bridget started singing When Irish Eyes Are Smiling as she boarded the plane. "Now that's good crazy," said Cathleen, and Aiden laughed and agreed.

The next day, Cathleen asked Aiden if he could stick around awhile and maybe go to the park with her. His aunt was on her way to work, so he agreed. On the way, they found a vendor and got a hot dog and a drink, and they found a bench and ate before Cathleen opened up to Aiden. He knew her well enough to see that something was bothering her again, so he sat quietly and listened.

"You remember me introducing Darcy as my mother's sister?"

"Yes," Aiden said.

"Well, she *is* my mother's sister—or at least she was what I thought was my mother's sister. It's complicated, but I just found out in Ireland that Darcy is my real mother." She then explained about the mother, who had raised her, having a miscarriage. When she found out she was unable to have more children, she became depressed. Darcy had come over to help her. She told him about the affair, what it had done to the family, and that the two families had not spoken for years—but since she returned home, they were trying to make peace with each other.

"So all these years, I thought Margaret was my mother, and because she raised me, she really was. She was just not my biological mother. Darcy is." She told him how Darcy attempted suicide and that when Cathleen went back to Ireland and found her in a rehabilitation center, Darcy had made a miraculous recovery. She said one of her grandfather Charlie's last wishes was for her to find her mother, and she had.

Aiden was just sitting there, trying to take it all in, knowing that God had had His hand in this all along. He didn't have anything to do with the fire, but He took something bad and made something wonderful of it. He told her they would both have to pray for these two families and ask God to continue to help them to understand what a blessing it would be to both families if they united.

"Both families have a granddaughter now, and they should be celebrating that" Aiden said as he put his arms around her. "God bless you for having to go through this and holding it all in as well as you have. Only He could give you the strength to do it."

"Yes, and He did," she said. "I am so thankful to have someone like you in my life. Thank you for being here when I needed you. You're just another one of God's blessings." As they got up to leave, Aiden hugged her again and thanked her for caring enough to share this with him.

When Cathleen returned to the shelter, there was a note and a phone number for her to call her father's family. Grandfather Charlie had had another stroke, and the prognosis did not look good. They said he had asked for her. Cathleen knew she had to take the next plane out if she wanted to see him alive, so she called Aiden and explained the situation and asked if he could get her to the airport. She would have to fly standby, but under the circumstances, the people at the airport pushed to get her on the next flight. It was almost midnight before she boarded the plane, and Aiden stayed until the plane took off.

Bridget met her at the airport, and they went straight to the hospital. Their grandfather was in the ICU, and the family let her go in next. He was on oxygen, but alert enough to know his granddaughter Cathleen was there. She held his hand, and he asked her if she had found her mother. "Bridget took me to see her, and I thank you for letting me know so I could." She told her grandfather what fun they had had when Bridget and Darcy had come to her graduation.

He told her he loved her and was glad she had been able to come back. He asked her if the family had all gotten right with the Lord, and she said, "Yes, grandfather, I believe we all have." She kissed him on his forehead, and told him she loved him as she was leaving the ICU. The last thing she heard him say was "Thank you, Lord."

The family was called in the next morning and told he had passed away peacefully in the night. A wake was held and many wonderful things were said about the man who was a friend to everyone he met. Funeral plans were arranged to have the service at the Catholic Church the family attended. The choir sang On Eagles Wings, and his favorite song, Going Home, was played with bagpipes. The church was overflowing, as he was a well-respected man and loved by many.

Everyone was in a somber mood after Grandfather Charlie's passing. Bridget wanted to take Cathleen by her house to eat before taking her to the Murphys'. Bridget's mom, Kerry, had a meal ready for the family, and she sat down to eat with them. She was tired and not really hungry but ate what she could out of respect. Her grandmother Myrna told her how the Murphys had visited them, given their condolences, and apologized for all the hard feelings over the years. They wanted to be able to be a part of Cathleen's life now. Too many years had gone by with animosity between the two families, and while they couldn't take it back, they could now look forward to the future. They were even all going back to the same church. That was a miracle in itself! Cathleen said she would be leaving soon, but promised to stay in touch.

As Cathleen was making plans to come home, she learned from Bridget that Darcy was having health problems again and was having difficulty walking. The two had become close since their trip to the States. She knew her suicide attempt had nothing to do with the disease her sister, Margaret, had had, but the depression had driven Darcy over the edge.

Darcy was afraid she wouldn't get to see her daughter again and asked for Cathleen, so her grandmother asked Cathleen if she could stay. How could she not? She had taken care of her mother for seven years and knew what to do, so of course she would stay. She needed to cancel her flight and let Aiden know, so she called to tell him. He said he understood and added, "Maybe my aunt and I can come over before I start college. Then we can visit and I can meet the whole family."

"I think you know by now what you're getting yourself into, so that would be great!"

She was glad she had remembered to bring her mom and dad's ashes. It gave her a sense of peace to know they would finally get back to the place they both had come from.

Chapter 14

Bridget had a new convertible, and things had not changed much with her driving. She took Cathleen to stay with her mother's family. They didn't live that far apart, but she ate a lot of dust before they got to the Murphys'.

When Cathleen saw Darcy in the wheelchair again, it brought back sad memories of the mother who had raised her. It was hard to watch two people she loved go through this terrible disease, even though her mom had died from other causes.

It was so different at the Murphys' this time. They didn't act like the same people; they were actually nice. "Thank you, Jesus," Cathleen said under her breath as she greeted and hugged everyone again. Kaitlin had grown like a weed and reminded Cathleen of herself at that age. Cathleen would be staying in a room with Darcy. She had not gotten used to calling her *Mom* yet, but hoped it would come with time spent with her. Darcy had a large room with twin beds and her own bathroom. Cathleen's bed was by the front window, and she could look out at all the pretty flowers and trees. Darcy wanted to sit up and talk awhile, so Cathleen made her comfortable with pillows behind her head in her lounge chair. She wanted to know how Aiden was, what had happened in New York since they had left, and whether she had chosen a college.

Cathleen answered Darcy's questions as best she could, and when Darcy started yawning, Cathleen knew it was time for bed. She helped to put her gown on and tucked Darcy in.

"I'm going to read my Bible for a while, but if you need anything, please let me know," Cathleen said.

"Would you read some to me?" Darcy asked.

Cathleen opened up her Bible to Romans 5, and as she read through the ninth verse, she noticed Darcy had drifted off with a smile still on her face. Tears slid down Cathleen's face as she thought of the times she had read that same chapter and verses to the mother who raised her, and what peace it had given her to know how much God loved her. Cathleen hoped it gave Darcy that same peace. She and her sister must have been close growing up for Darcy to come to the States to help take care of her. Cathleen prayed before she slipped under her covers: "Thank You, Lord, for giving me two wonderful mothers and for showing me how great your love is."

Cathleen had left the curtains open that night before going to bed so she could wake up with the light and could enjoy the view of the countryside from the second story. When she awoke the next morning, she looked over at Darcy and saw she was looking back at her.

"How long have you been awake?" Cathleen asked

"Not long," Darcy said. "I have to go to the loo, but I didn't want to wake you."

"Well, don't you ever worry about waking me up for anything, especially that! I'm here to help you, so let's get you to the toilet before it's too late," said Cathleen.

Cathleen helped Darcy get ready for the day and they went down to breakfast. The days started early here, and the meals were at the same time each day. After breakfast, they cleared the table, and Darcy wanted to go outside. They had several acres of land on their property. There were trails around the house where Darcy used to ride her bike. She was still able to do some things on her own but had the wheelchair for safety reasons. Darcy still had her bike and let Cathleen use it. She needed it to keep up with Darcy.

There was a stream down one of the trails, and Darcy told Cathleen that she and Margaret would take their shoes off and sit on the bank with their feet in the water when they were younger. She said Daniel used to come over, and she had seen him and Margaret doing the same thing. She caught them kissing one day, but she couldn't tell anyone because the Murphys and the O'Connors didn't get along. They were still holding grudges over the land back then. Darcy was sweet on Daniel too, but she was younger than her sister and was considered a nuisance. She couldn't say she wished she had stayed a nuisance, because there would be no Cathleen. She loved her daughter too much to call her a mistake. It was almost like déjà vu sitting here with her daughter. "Guess we better get back before they think we ran away," Darcy said, and she led them back down the path to the house.

Daniel had come over for a visit after Cathleen was born, but he had never talked about what happened. He had secretly gone to see Darcy to give her a picture of their daughter, because he thought she would never get to see what she looked like otherwise. In fact, they met at the same stream where he and Margaret used to meet—and now Cathleen and Darcy had gone there.

It was years later that Darcy had tried to take her life, but she couldn't even do that right. Her mam said it was because God had His hand on her, and it wasn't her time. Darcy had kept a lot of things to herself over the years but had finally gone over to the O'Connors and confessed to Daniel's parents about what had happened between them and asked for their forgiveness. Charles had hugged her and said, "To err is human; to forgive divine." Myrna had always blamed Darcy for what had happened, but knew she had to forgive her, and she did.

Chapter 15

Darcy seemed to be doing better every day. Cathleen had been thinking about starting a horse ranch here. She remembered her ride with her grandfather and how relaxing it was to ride through the countryside. She thought about the horse ranches back home that helped people cope with their injuries and disabilities, and thought that might be good for her mom. She would talk to both families and get their opinion on starting one here with these services. When Cathleen approached them, they liked the idea and agreed to donate time and money and make this a joint effort. She knew she didn't have all the skills needed yet, but she was willing to learn—and maybe she could get some good legal advice from the lawyer Grandfather Charlie had used. He was an old family friend and knew many influential people. There was a lot more to this than she had realized, but God had a way of taking a mustard seed and turning it into something big, so she was going to rely on Him.

In two months' time, they were able to get the land cleared, a barn built with stables for the horses, and an area fenced off for some of the animals. There was a hen house, but the dogs and cats were able to run loose. They only had room for six mares and four colts, so they would start with that.

Cathleen started taking Darcy over, and they rode the trails together before the family opened the ranch to the public and hired experienced riders to help train the staff. Once the lawyer had gotten everything approved for her, they would be able to open. Aunt Cara's triplets said they would come and help after school and on weekends. They loved being able to brush the horses, but not so much cleaning out their stalls!

Being around other people seemed to help raise Darcy's spirits. Cathleen was enjoying watching the kids and other people come out to ride. Even if their health didn't improve, their moods did, and that was an important step to recovery. It was satisfying to see both families working together.

Cathleen was wondering if she would be able to go back home soon when she started noticing little signs with Darcy that she had seen with her mother. Darcy wasn't as talkative as before, and Cathleen wondered whether she was taking her medication. She would find Darcy staring at her, and when Cathleen would say, "What's wrong? Do you need something?" Darcy would just shake her head no and smile. Cathleen talked to her grandmother about getting her mom a doctor's appointment, so she made one for the following week. Darcy's mom took her in for a physical, and Cathleen went with her. The doctor said he couldn't be sure if her problems were from the disease or the depression, but they both seemed to go together. She was supposed to still be on her antidepressants, but Darcy didn't think she needed them, so she hid them until she could flush them down the toilet. Cathleen was unaware of this and couldn't understand why her mom had taken a turn for the worse so quickly.

Cathleen had to put college on hold before she left the States, but she decided to talk to Bridget about taking some courses online. She thought she could start building up her credits that way, and then she wouldn't be so far behind when she did get to go home. Capable people were running the horse ranch now, and they were doing well enough that she didn't have to go out there so often anymore.

Bridget had a computer and told Cathleen she could come over and use it anytime. She thought about it and decided to invest in her own laptop so she could be with her mother. She called Bridget and asked if she would take her to buy one. She explained to Darcy that Bridget was going to take her shopping, and tears started to trickle down Darcy's cheeks. Cathleen leaned over, hugged her, and said, "Oh, Mom, I'll be back. I promise!" Cathleen hadn't realized what she had said, but she had known for some time that Darcy was her only mom now. Even if Cathleen didn't pronounce it the way the Irish did, Darcy understood and said, "I know you will."

Darcy started back on her antidepressants, and seemed to be improving again but was still having some problems walking. Now that she had her daughter, she didn't want to let go of life and was really struggling to live.

Cathleen was making progress on her courses on the computer, but it would take several years to get her degree. Every course she could get done was a step ahead for when she got home. She would work on them for hours every night.

She was still reading the Bible to Darcy every night before she went to sleep, and one night Darcy said, "I know I was baptized by the Catholic Church, but I want to be immersed in the river like John the Baptist baptized Jesus."

"Okay," Cathleen said. "You know the Catholics don't do that as a rule, but we can certainly ask them to. We will have to talk to the priest first to see if it can be done. Can you wait until then?"

"Yes," Darcy said.

Cathleen got to church early Sunday morning to speak to the priest. The priest said he thought it odd that Darcy wanted to be baptized again, but since she was so adamant about being immersed in the river, and since everyone in her family was a faithful parishioner, he would make an exception. There was a river not far from the church, so that afternoon, family and some church members attended Darcy's baptism, and they were all invited back to the Murphys' house for lunch. Darcy had such a peaceful look about her now, and Cathleen was glad the church had allowed her mom this one request.

Later that day, Cathleen asked her father's family if she could have permission to sprinkle her dad's ashes over Grandfather Charlie's grave. They were glad she had brought them back, and everyone went to the cemetery with her. The priest also came and said a few words. He spoke of "dust to dust, ashes to ashes" and then read a passage from 1 Corinthians 15:55. The ceremony seemed to bring the O'Connors some closure. Even though there had been a memorial service back in the States, there had been no family to attend and no body to bury. That was why Cathleen had brought their remains to Ireland. She felt like that was what her parents would have wanted.

Chapter 16

It had been quiet around the Murphy house since the baptism. Darcy seemed to be at peace but had no desire to go for rides down by the stream lately. She still liked to sit on the porch with the family in the evening and listen to them play and sing. Sometimes Cathleen could hear Darcy singing along with them. Her favorite song was Amazing Grace.

Kaitlin was getting to be quite the entertainer. What she didn't learn from her family, she had been learning at school, and she loved to show off her talent. Kaitlin's mother, Clara, was Darcy's sister. Clara was separated from her husband, and though Kaitlin did not have a father figure around, she had lots of love from the family. They all doted on her and said that if she wasn't careful, she could end up like her cousin Bridget. But she loved her cousin! Everyone in her family thought Bridget might be a bad influence, but Kaitlin thought she was just adventurous.

The family tried to keep a tight rein on Kaitlin by getting her involved in sports and music. She often missed the school bus and had to depend on someone to bring her home. She had many suitors but wasn't really interested in anything but having fun, and since boys always seemed to get jealous, she never got serious with anyone. She loved the horse ranch and recruited a few of her friends to come on weekends to help. The business had grown, and the barn was expanded to accommodate more horses. The other animals had already multiplied in number.

It had been awhile since Cathleen had heard from Aiden, so she tried to reach him. He was at the food bank and could only talk for a few minutes. She told him about the horse ranch and said she had thought of a name for it—Happy Acres Ranch Inc., because of the two mothers who had made her so happy. He said he liked the name and that he would be happy when she came home. She told him she had been practicing basketball and would take him up on a game when she got home. Kaitlin played too, and Cathleen asked her if they could play one afternoon after school. Bridget dropped her off at Kaitlin's school gym and went to see her brother, William, at his pub. He worked all the time, so that was the only way she could visit with him. Cathleen said to give them an hour and come back. She thought she would have Kaitlin worn out by then, but it turned out to be the opposite! This girl had been holding out on her. Kaitlin had been playing with the boys and had learned a thing or two that she could teach Cathleen. She had second thoughts about taking Aiden on now!

When Bridget picked the girls up, she told them she would love an American hamburger, so they stopped at an American fast food chain. It was dark by the time they headed home. Riding with Bridget in the daylight was scary enough, but Kaitlin loved it, so Cathleen let her have the front seat while she scrunched down in the back. "Remind me to be home before dark from now on," Cathleen said very loudly. That just made Bridget drive faster, and Kaitlin laughed most of the way home.

When they got home, Grandma Deidre said "Darcy wasn't feeling well and kept asking for you." Cathleen went into their room, and Darcy was curled up in bed, moaning. "What's wrong, Mom?" Cathleen asked.

"I don't know. I'm hurting."

"Where?" Cathleen asked, but Darcy couldn't say. Her mom had given her the pain medicine she took when things got bad, which she took and finally calmed down. Cathleen stayed by Darcy's side until she went to sleep. She wondered if her going off had affected Darcy, but she had seemed to be okay when Cathleen left.

She thought of Aiden again and knew she needed to call him and give him the address here. She had been so preoccupied with things that she had neglected to call. She hadn't thought to give him her address when she last talked to him. The time zone was different here, but she would call and leave the information if she couldn't reach him.

When Cathleen didn't hear back from Aiden, she decided to call his aunt, hoping she was home and not sleeping. Fiona had worked the late shift, so she had just gotten home when the phone rang. She was happy to hear from Cathleen and asked how everyone was. Cathleen said they were all fine except for her mom, who was having a bad day. She apologized for not writing or calling sooner but said she had lots of things to deal with in Ireland and had started taking college courses online. When she asked about Aiden, Fiona told her he had flown to California to check out the college he would be attending. One of his friends lived in San Diego, and he was spending a few days there before flying back.

Fiona told her they both planned to fly to Ireland in a couple of weeks and needed her address —and Cathleen explained that she was calling for that very reason. After they hung up, Aiden called. He told her he was visiting a friend in San Diego, but would be seeing her soon. She felt happy to have finally heard from him, and now she could look forward to their visit. Cathleen wondered why Aiden had not mentioned applying at a college in California.

Even though Darcy was feeling better, Cathleen decided to take her to the doctor for a checkup. He said it was not unusual for someone in her condition to have these episodes every so often. They could come and go for a long time. The good news was that Darcy was holding her own right now. Cathleen's worries for her eased and she could concentrate on her college assignments. She knew she couldn't leave her mother just yet.

Now she had Aiden's visit to look forward to, and she was counting the days until they would be here. Kilkenny wasn't that far away, so they should be able to see each other often. She was glad Aiden had met her biological mother while her health was still good. Now that both sides of her family were getting along, she would have no problem introducing him to them.

Cathleen got a call from Aiden saying they were in Kilkenny now and would see her in a few days. It seemed like a long time had passed since they had seen each other, even though it had only been two months. Aiden called a few days later and invited her to visit his family. He was borrowing his brother's car and would be picking her up at 5:00 p.m. She would wear the nice dress she had bought with the girls in New York. She explained to her mom that Aiden was in town and she would be gone for a few hours, but she would still read the Bible to her when she got back if she was still up. Darcy understood, and said, "Have a good time."

The apple hadn't fallen very far from the tree in the case of Aiden's father, Derek, and his brother, Kevin, who was two years older. The whole family was as nice as could be. They liked to pull jokes on each other, so when Aiden brought Cathleen into their home, they had all dressed up like a bunch of hillbillies—his parents had even blacked out a few of their teeth! Fiona gave them away when she started laughing and said, "What are you trying to do, run the poor girl off?" The joke was on them then, so they all laughed and cleaned up. Cathleen offered to help Abigail and Fiona set up the food buffet style. She had never seen so much food in her life as she had in Ireland. With her mother being sick since she was ten, she had done the best she could after school, but it was meager compared to the way they ate here. She wasn't that good of a cook, because she had never had anyone to teach her.

Aiden wanted to show Cathleen around his city, so he borrowed his brother's car again and gave her a tour. He showed her the elementary school he had gone to, where he had played football and basketball as a kid, and the movie theatre where he had taken in a matinee every Saturday before leaving Ireland. They went into the candy store he had gone to as a child, and he couldn't leave without buying her some of his favorite fudge made with real cream and butter, and loaded with nuts. On the drive back, he told her how much he had missed her, and she admitted she had missed him too.

"I wish I could say how long I will be here, but I don't know."

She told him she was taking classes online and was ahead in a lot of her courses because she had nothing else to do while she helped take care of her mother. He was surprised to hear her call Darcy her mother but was glad Cathleen had reconciled with her.

Aiden had only two days left in Ireland, so they spent as much time together as possible. Aiden never mentioned why he went to California, so she never brought the subject up because of her fear of losing him. Cathleen talked Darcy into going down to the stream with them and showing Aiden where her parents used to hang out a lot. They all took their shoes off and dangled their feet in the icy water. It would be the last time Cathleen went down there with her mother.

Bridget wanted to take him and his aunt to the airport, so Aiden's family all said good-bye to Aiden and Fiona at their door. Cathleen had already warned Aiden about her cousin's driving, but he wanted to experience it for himself. They got to the airport with time to spare, and Aiden leaned over to Cathleen and said, "You were so right. This woman should have been a race car driver!"

"I heard that," Bridget said. "My family wouldn't let me. Do you think I'm too old now? I could probably make more money racing than doing hair!"

"Don't quit your day job," said Cathleen.

They sat in the lobby talking while waiting for Aiden and Fiona's plane to board. They all agreed they should do this more often. "Maybe when we're all educated and rich," Bridget said, laughing at the thought of that happening. It didn't hurt to have rich grandparents, though! They all hugged before Aiden and Fiona boarded the plane, and in unison, they said, "We'll see you soon!"

Chapter 17

The ride back was quiet. Cathleen believed she was falling in love with Aiden, but Bridget had already figured that out. As they pulled in to the Murphys' driveway, Kaitlin came running out and said they couldn't find Darcy. Cathleen immediately thought of where she had probably gone. She loved to go down to the trails where the stream was, but had not gone alone lately. She had trouble maneuvering her chair down that path now, and Cathleen wondered why Darcy would attempt to go there alone. Cathleen looked into their room first before pulling the bicycle from the shed and taking off down the path they always followed.

When she got there, she had the shock of her life. Her mother had wheeled herself too close to the stream. She must have hit one of the boulders as she fell, because her chair had flipped over, and she was face down in the water. She had not been able to pick herself up or turn over, so she had drowned in her favorite place. Cathleen pulled her out of the water and saw where she had hit her head. She called 999, the emergency number there, while performing CPR to no avail. An ambulance came and rushed her to the hospital. The coroner pronounced her dead and ruled her death an accident.

Everyone was in shock. Cathleen knew she would never have tried to take her life a second time, because she knew Jesus and the Bible better now and knew it was wrong.

She was buried in the dress and shoes they had bought in New York and Cathleen put her new handbag in her hand. She would go out of this world in style and reach the other one in peace and comfort—and her sister, Margaret, and Daniel would be there waiting for her. Bridget and Cathleen wore the dresses they had bought that day in New York in memory of their time there. The service was held at their family church. Her favorite song, Amazing Grace, was sung by the choir.

There was no peace for the family this time, only sadness. Cathleen had now lost two mothers through tragic accidents, and Grandma Deidre had lost two daughters. She took her mother Margaret's ashes and sprinkled them over Darcy's grave. They would be together forever now. She called Aiden and gave him the sad news and said she would be coming home. Could he pick her up?

Aiden noticed the sadness was back in Cathleen's eyes when she got into the car, but this time he understood why. He dreaded telling her of his plans to go to pre-med school in California. He had hoped he could get her to move there too, but after finding out she was looking for an apartment, he knew that wasn't going to happen now. He hadn't known his aunt had already told Cathleen his plans. Cathleen didn't see how it could work out for them anyway, so a few days later she went over to his aunt's and told Aiden that since she didn't know what the future would bring with her health, they should go their separate ways.

"Aren't you being a little premature about this?" Aiden asked. "You don't even know you carry the gene, and it's highly unlikely you do. You already know how I feel about you, and want to marry you. I'll wait a year for you, but only a year. That's a year wasted without you, as far as I'm concerned."

Cathleen chose not to go to the airport with his aunt to see Aiden off. Sometimes he just did not understand her. Why would she rather wait for years, never knowing when and if she would develop the disease? He was a patient man, and he knew she loved him, but he could only wait so long. He knew she was just scared of the future. For him, love could overcome all obstacles, but he didn't seem to be able to convince her. Maybe time apart would.

Cathleen had enrolled in New York University earlier and transferred her credits online. It should put her a year ahead. Her good grades gave her some advantage and a scholarship. She chose an apartment close to the college and put a deposit down. She put all her efforts into making the best grades and finishing college so she could do what she felt called to do. She thought she should have several good years left if the disease should come her way.

One evening, while helping a family, Maria ran into her at the food bank, where Cathleen volunteered when she had free time. Cathleen told her she had taken college courses on line while she was in Ireland, and wanted to get her master's in social work. Maria said she was going to law school to be an advocate for children's rights and said they needed to hook up with each other after college. They both agreed it would be wonderful to work together. They exchanged phone numbers and said they would stay in touch.

Chapter 18

Cathleen moved into her new apartment on her eighteenth birthday. She had changed her mailing address from the shelter to her new apartment, and already had mail arriving in her mailbox, including birthday cards from Ireland and one from Aiden. He had planned to buy her an engagement ring on her birthday, but he knew she wouldn't accept it now.

Bridget wrote in her card that she had some ideas rolling around in her head and wanted to call her and talk to her about them. *Oh goodness,* she thought, *surely she doesn't want to be a race car driver here! I better call her right away and squash that idea quickly.* Bridget let out one of her boisterous laughs when Cathleen shared her worry.

"No, that's not it at all. I was thinking of opening a delicatessen with a small bakery there in New York."

"Well, that's certainly different," Cathleen said. "We have a deli on just about every corner here."

"But you don't have an Irish one, do you?" Bridget said.

"Well, not that I can recall."

Bridget went on to tell her she wanted to collect all the great recipes from both sides of the family and name each product after each member. She had the money saved to do it and had already gotten her family's approval and help if needed.

This is just what New York needs—more crazy people, thought Cathleen, but kept her thoughts to herself. "If this is what you want to do in life, Bridget, follow your dream. That's what I'm doing."

"It will take me about six weeks to figure this all out, and then I'll call you when I'm ready to come. I'm leaving my car with Kaitlin, with her promise not to wreck it. By the way, do you have room for me to stay with you until I can get my own place?"

"Of course. You can stay as long as you need to."

"Thanks, cousin," said Bridget and hung up.

"What have I got myself into?" Cathleen asked herself. Maybe it would take her six months instead of six weeks to get ready. She loved her cousin—it was just hard to be serious around her, and serious was what she was all about right now. She was staying busy with her studies and helping out at the food bank. Marie came by to visit her often, and Cathleen talked her into volunteering at the food bank in her spare time.

The time just seemed to fly by. It had only been six weeks since she had heard from Bridget when she received her letter. Everything was in place. Bridget had looked online at a few buildings to rent but didn't want to make a decision until she could see them in person. Would it be okay for her to come next week? That girl! She had already told her she could come. She just wasn't expecting her so soon. Cathleen called her that night and left a message telling her to just let her know what flight she was taking and what time she'd arrive. The time zone and busy schedules made it hard for them to talk.

Bridget got a ticket on a late flight out and left a message for Cathleen. Cathleen saw Maria at the food bank and told her about her cousin coming, and that she was lots of fun. Maria said she couldn't wait to meet her and was excited to hear about the delicatessen. Maria's mom loved to cook and bake, so maybe she could quit her housekeeping job and help Bridget. Cathleen said that was a possibility—if her mom could handle her cousin.

Cathleen finally broke down and bought herself a car. It was hard trying to get to all the places she needed to go without one. She bought a mini SUV and thought it was big enough for her needs. When she arrived at the terminal, Bridget was already waiting outside. They were barely able to get her luggage in the back. Cathleen wasn't prepared for the huge amount of luggage Bridget had brought.

"Why didn't you ship it?"

"I did ship most of my stuff."

There goes my closet space, thought Cathleen. *What am I going to do with this girl?*

"What fun we're going to have here in America, cousin!" Bridget said as she looked at the big city.

"Yes, and good luck finding your way around the Big Apple while I'm in school."

Bridget, of course, wanted to look at the places that she had found online right away. Therefore, on Saturday, Cathleen gave in and chauffeured her around New York to look for a good location for her deli. The ones she saw online were too far off the beaten path, so they headed back to the condo. On the way back, Bridget spotted a restaurant that had closed up and had a small For Rent sign hanging on the door. "Stop here please. Let's see if we can check this one out. "Cathleen pulled around the corner and parked. They saw some men moving counters from the back of the store, so Bridget hurried over to see if they would let them look at the inside of the shop.

One of the men was the previous owner of the restaurant and he took them inside to look. It had been a Chinese place previously, and had not done very well. There were too many already he said. The space was quite large. He said it had always been too big for him, but the price had been right. Bridget took the owner of the building's phone number down and asked what they were going to do with their equipment. "We'll try to sell them at the flea market," he said.

"Why don't you sell them to me so you don't have to move them?" she asked. That was fine with him, so they moved them back in, and Bridget added, "Since you don't have to move them off, and I'm paying you cash, what kind of deal can we make?" Bridget pulled out a wad of cash, and they made a deal on the spot.

"You should have been here when I bought my car," Cathleen said.

"You should have called me. I can deal on the phone too. My granddaddy was good at it and he taught me well."

"He didn't teach you to drive like you do."

"No, my mam did."

Bridget called the owner, and true to her word, she got a deal on the space, leasing it for two years. She found needed specialty vendors, and the next step was to hire workers. Cathleen told her about Maria's mother and said she would be good at working in the bakery. She told Bridget that she would ask Maria if her mother would be available.

They decided to have dinner at one of the other delis in town to see what their competition might be, but it was no match for Bridget's food. She had her family's recipes for shepherd's pie, Irish lamb stew, and Irish soda bread, along with many other specialties. She was using her own version of Dublin coddle, which consisted of bacon with sausage, potatoes, and onion. The desserts were to die for, and the food guaranteed to put inches on your waistline.

They drove by the food bank on the way home so Cathleen could show her what she did in her spare time. "This is nice," Bridget said once they were inside. "This is what Darcy would have loved to do." They looked at each other and Cathleen said "Like mother, like daughter"—but not without a tear or two sliding down her cheeks. The pain of losing her so soon after she had found her was still raw.

Chapter 19

The year seemed to fly, and Cathleen didn't know where the time had gone. She had spoken on the phone to Aiden's aunt, who said Aiden was doing well and focusing on his studies. When Cathleen asked if he was coming home for a visit, Fiona said, "Yes, he asked me to call you and tell you he was coming in for the weekend and would like to see you." Cathleen gave Fiona her new address and phone number. She said she missed them and would love to see them both.

Saturday morning, Aiden called and woke her up. He said he was coming over and bringing coffee and Irish rolls from a new bakery in town. She didn't know if he was kidding her or if he knew Bridget was here. The doorbell rang ten minutes later, and Cathleen had just managed to grab a T-shirt and jeans and pull a comb through her hair. He just stood at the door looking at her, and she laughed and said, "Well, come on in before the coffee gets cold!"

He laid the bag on the table and hugged her. "Just look at you—pretty even right out of bed!"

She blushed and said, "I'm starving, let's eat!" He had a couple of sausages to go with the rolls, and they didn't talk much until they were gone.

"Were you teasing me, or did you know Bridget had opened up the delicatessen?"

"I knew," he said. "We've talked a few times since she came back. Have you thought any more about you and me? You know I love you, but I can't wait much longer for you to decide whether you want to be with me or not. I think you are being paranoid about having the disease, but if you do, I will take care of you just like you did both of your moms. It won't change the way I feel about you."

"I'm just so confused by all that has happened in the last eighteen months and so afraid of losing you too. I don't want to be a burden to you. It would hurt your chances of a good career, and I don't want to do that. I don't want the disease, but if I knew I was carrying the gene, I would not be able to function as well as I am now. Don't you understand that?"

"No, I don't, because love has no boundaries. Either you love me or you don't. I want to marry you, woman—don't you know that?"

"I promised myself I would not marry until I knew whether I carried the gene."

"It's already been a year, and I can't wait that long!"

"Can we wait until I finish college?"

"I think you're just making excuses. I can't wait forever. When you come to your senses, let me know. In the meantime, I have to live my life, and if it means dating other girls, I will. You know I'll always love you no matter what."

"I know," she said, wiping tears from her eyes. They hugged, not knowing when or even if they would see each other again. When he left, she curled up into a ball on the sofa and cried until there were no more tears left. "Dear Lord," she prayed, "what am I doing so wrong? Why am I hurting myself so much when I know I love him, but just can't make the commitment yet? Please help me to get through this and make the right decision."

She had to quit feeling sorry for herself, so she got up, showered, and dressed to go down to the food bank. Aiden had been the one to get her involved in it, and she was glad he did, because it was therapy for her.

She decided to run by the deli first and see how things were going. Bridget's new sign, Bridget's Irish Deli and Bakery had been put up and she had hired a couple of people to work the deli and tend to the register. Maria's mom, Lupe, had quit her cleaning job and was now working in the bakery. Cathleen told Bridget about Aiden coming by, but she already knew, and could tell by Cathleen's look that things didn't go well for them.

"You're crazier than I am if you let him go, Cat. You're going to lose him to someone else if you wait too long."

"Thanks for reminding me again," Cathleen said. She went over, greeted Lupe, and picked up some baked goods to take to the volunteers at the food bank. The day went by quickly as she sorted and made bags of food ready for those who came by. At the end of the day, she was ready to go home and work on her college courses. Maybe the sooner she graduated, the better she would feel about making decisions.

She set her clock early enough on Sunday to get up and go to church. It made her feel good to see all her friends there. She hadn't been sure Aiden was still in town, but he was there with his aunt. She had to find out from Bridget that he was flying out later in the day.

"You sure do know a lot more about Aiden than I do now."

"That's because Aiden and I still talk to each other. You're not jealous, are you? I'd go for him myself if I didn't know how much he loved you. But I'm not his type."

"Suit yourself," Cathleen said as she left the church.

She was determined not to let this get her down. She wanted to get her schooling out of the way as soon as possible and to start working with children and families in crisis. She had talked to Mr. Henderson, the owner of the food bank, and he said he had plenty of space there she could use as an office. He also owned the building where Bridget had her deli. He was a nice Christian man and well thought of in the community.

The more she thought of what she had done with the ranch in Ireland, the more she thought it would work here. Mr. Henderson had more land outside of the city, and she wondered if he might collaborate with her on this next venture. He was all about good causes, and he may not have thought of this one. She needed to talk to Maria, because she would need a good lawyer.

Chapter 20

Another year had passed before Cathleen realized it. She had been asked out many times over the year, but she always had an excuse as to why she couldn't go. Oh, she had had lunch with a few of her male college friends, but that was all there was to it. Unfortunately, Aiden had taken her heart with him, and she couldn't get it back. She had been working hard to get her degree as a licensed social worker. Maybe then she could think more clearly about their relationship.

In the meantime, Cathleen's and Maria's offices were being set up at the food bank. Cathleen was thinking of going back to Ireland for a visit. It had been a year since she had been, and both grandmothers and her one living grandfather were not getting any younger. They heard that Kaitlin was doing very well in her drama and vocal classes and that she wanted to try her luck in Hollywood when she graduated from high school. The girl wasn't thinking straight. She didn't know anyone in Hollywood and had no earthly idea what an undertaking like that might involve. Someone definitely needed to straighten her out!

Cathleen talked Bridget into taking a quick flight back to Ireland with her to see the family and check on the ranch there. It seemed both families were doing better than Cathleen could have ever imagined. Bridget's bother, William, had sold his pub and was now working on the ranch with the animals. He had always wanted to work with horses, and he loved taking children out on the trails. Two of the mares had had foals, and now the barn needed an addition. The donations were still coming in. Parents were bringing their children with injuries and disabilities, and some people just came for the love of riding. Most of the visitors always left a donation, but there was never a set fee. They gave from their hearts what they could afford, and those who couldn't didn't have to.

The days passed quickly, and they headed home late Sunday night. Bridget and Cathleen had talked to Kaitlin about coming to New York, and told her she would be great at helping them out, and she could still pursue her acting and singing career. She did love working with the people at the ranch there, and said she would think it over. She was having second thoughts about going to Hollywood anyway, and she thought she might be able to get on with a production company there in New York if she decided to make the move.

Before Cathleen got up the following morning, her phone rang, and it was Aiden's aunt. She asked about their trip, and Cathleen told her how well the ranch was doing.

"The reason I'm calling you is to let you know something before you hear it from someone else," Fiona said. "Aiden called and said he was engaged to someone from California." Cathleen said she couldn't really blame him. He deserved to be happy, and even though her heart was not so happy, she told Fiona to tell him she wished him health and happiness.

Cathleen decided to get busy making the American ranch a reality. She talked at length with Mr. Henderson and showed him videos of the ranch in Ireland. He was very much interested in becoming a partner. He hadn't made it known as yet, but he was also very interested in her. He owned eighty acres out of the city in New Jersey and thought it would be a great place for a horse ranch. There were trees that needed clearing, but that was not a problem for Geoffrey Henderson. He knew just about every company in town and could get the job done quickly.

Cathleen had plans drawn up and wanted to start with two stables this time and a large recreation room. Trails were being made while some of the land was being cleared. They both thought Happy Acres Ranch Inc. would be a good name for both ranches. She thought both of her mothers would approve. They would want the ranches to be a happy place, and so far they were. She would see about having a sign made and advertising it when it was near completion.

Mr. Henderson insisted on her calling him Geoffrey and kept asking Cathleen out. They had been out to eat several times. However, they usually talked about business. That's all Cathleen was really interested in talking about. She missed Aiden so much, but knew she could not talk to him now. She wondered whom he was engaged to. Since he was in California, she wasn't hearing any rumors. *Maybe I can get Bridget to find out,* she thought. That girl could get a secret out of a deaf-mute.

Cathleen decided to drop by the bakery. She spoke to Lupe and the new girl they had hired and went back to Bridget's office. She was just finishing a phone order, and Cathleen sat down for a quick chat. She asked how the business was doing, and Bridget beamed as she said, "It couldn't be any better. These New Yorkers were starved for some good Irish food." Bridget asked how things were going with her and Geoffrey. Apparently, rumors were already flying around about them.

"We are not a couple, Bridget. We simply go out to lunch and dinner sometimes—and talk business, if it's any of yours!"

"Hold onto your horses, cuz, and don't be so snippy with me. I'm just trying to make sure you don't make a big mistake."

"Like what?" Cathleen said.

"Like falling for the wrong guy when you know there's someone in California who still loves you."

"But he's engaged now!" she replied.

"And whose fault is that? He gave you more time than most men would, and you jumped the fence and ran. Besides, I hear he's not very happy out West and would like to come back to the East Coast."

"What about his fiancée?" Cathleen asked.

"Well, that must not be going too well, either. It seems she still likes to party too much."

"Just who is she?"

"A nurse Aiden was working with."

"That figures," Cathleen mumbled.

Chapter 21

Maria stopped by the food bank to see Cathleen and their new offices. Geoffrey had already been there and had left to check on how the ranch was coming along.

"I'm taking my exam next week," Maria said, "and hopefully I will pass it the first time. Then I can get the ball rolling in the judiciary courts. Geoffrey seems like such a nice guy, don't you think?"

"Yes, he's a nice Christian man." Cathleen said.

"I heard you two were seeing each other."

"We've only had dinner dates to talk about business, Maria. We're not a couple."

"Oh," said Maria, "I thought you were both serious."

"Well, let's put it this way: I like him as a friend, but I'm not serious about him, so if you like him, please don't think you will hurt my feelings. He needs a nice young woman like you. No one can replace Aiden with me. I've never indicated to Geoffrey that there was anything but friendship between us. So if you like him, then let him know."

"Thank you—I was under the wrong impression."

"Just pray about it, Maria, and if you trust in God, He will steer you in the right direction." She thought about what she had just said and wondered why it didn't seem to be working for her. She knew what she wanted but was too afraid of her future to give in. Too bad she couldn't or wouldn't take her own advice. They hugged, and Cathleen went to the back to help get more bags of food ready for pick up. They would be delivering to some of the shut-ins today, and Cathleen was scheduled to ride with one of the drivers.

Geoffrey was back from the ranch when Cathleen returned from the deliveries. He told her everything was coming along slowly but surely. They were putting up the stables and had built a fenced area for some of the animals. His men had found a few horses for sale, and one was with foal. After they talked business, Geoffrey asked if she wanted to grab a bite to eat. "Not tonight, Geoffrey, but Maria is in her office—maybe you should invite her.

"I would have already, but I didn't know she was available. She's a beautiful girl. I was sure she already had someone special."

"She has been too busy going to law school to be involved with anyone lately, so here is your chance if you want it."

"What about you? Is there someone special in your life now?"

"There has been someone special in my life for the last five years. I have just been too stubborn to give in. No one will ever be able to replace him in my heart. Maybe once this new ranch is up and running, I will be able to make a decision one way or another. I just hope I haven't waited too long."

Geoffrey went back to Maria's office, and in a few minutes, she came out with her purse and a big smile on her face. "Geoffrey wants to know if you can close up tonight. We have a dinner date."

"No problem. You guys have a great time," Cathleen said as they left the building. *I hope everything works out between the two of them*, Cathleen thought. *They seem suited for one another.*

When Cathleen got home, Bridget wanted to know why she was so late. There was supposed to be a rule in place that they would call each other if they would be home later than usual. Cathleen had forgotten to call to let Bridget know she was closing, so she got a lecture. Sometimes they both slipped up, but neither one was used to having to answer to someone else.

"Guess who called while you were away?" asked Bridget.

"Was it the pope?" Cathleen asked, trying to be smart.

"Close, but guess again."

"Aiden," she said.

"No, but you are so close to being hot."

"Well, for goodness' sake, just tell me."

"Aiden's brother, Kevin. He's coming over to stay awhile with his aunt while Aiden is in California.

"I thought you told me Aiden was thinking about coming back here and finishing his internship."

"I did, but I didn't say when. Have you met Kevin?"

"Only once," said Cathleen.

Is he as cute as Aiden? Is he nice? Is he available?" Bridget wanted to know.

"Slow down, girl. I just met him when I went to his home. He looked like a hillbilly when I saw him."

"What do you mean, a hillbilly?"

Cathleen laughed and told her about Aiden's family pulling a joke on her by dressing up like hillbillies.

"Well, I'm sure to like him if he has a sense of humor. He sounded nice on the phone, so I'm anxious to meet him," Bridget said.

"I wish Kaitlin would make up her mind on what she wants to do. Then maybe they could travel together," said Cathleen. She hadn't heard from her cousin in a while and hoped she wasn't up to mischief.

It wasn't long before she heard from Kaitlin. She had been going over and playing and singing in one of her friend's pubs. That was not what Cathleen wanted to hear.

"You need to think about coming over and helping out on the ranch. You'll love it here, and you'll get introduced to some American culture. We could even have entertainment night where you could play and sing at the ranch."

"I'll think about it," Kaitlin said.

"Well, don't think too long. Aiden's brother is coming soon, and you two could catch the same flight."

Chapter 22

Things were in full swing at the new ranch, and the men were even putting up the new sign! So far they had four mares, two stallions, and two colts. One of the mares was ready to foal any day now. They were looking for another colt or two for the younger children to ride. The barn was big enough to hold the horses they had so far, but should the ranch be as successful as they hoped, it was a given that they would be building an addition.

Maria and Cathleen had their college degrees now, and were working out of their offices and building up clients for the state. They were both working on a case where, supposedly, an abused child was given back to the parents, and Cathleen was counseling the family. The case was complicated: the child said she fell down a lot, and the parents had denied abusing her, but such situations were common. Cathleen said she would get a pediatrician to examine the child, and she called the American Board of Pediatrics and asked for a recommendation. They said they had a new doctor in town whom everyone seemed to like. He was still an intern but came highly recommended. She asked for his name and number, and when she heard the name Aiden O'Leary, she was taken aback. She hadn't realized he had already returned.

"Miss O'Connor, are you still there?"

"Yes, I'm sorry. What did you say the number was?" When she hung up, she called Bridget and asked if she had known Aiden was in town.

"Yes, I did, and I also know his brother and Kaitlin are flying in next weekend."

"Well, thanks again for not sharing! When were you planning on telling me Aiden was here?"

"Oh, when I got around to it. He just called me this morning and told me he was here. He's been here a couple of weeks but had to find an apartment since his brother will be staying with his aunt now."

"Since you seem to know all the news, where will Kaitlin be staying?"

"She will stay with us, of course. She can bunk with me."

"Oh, no, that won't work. We bump into each other enough with one bathroom already. I will see about getting a three bedroom in our same building with two baths, and you two can share a bath and bump into each other then."

Cathleen had taken the little girl to see Aiden, and he had examined her and could not say whether there was abuse without more testing, after which Aiden called Cathleen and told her the girl's diagnosis. She had a rare form of osteoporosis that caused her bones to break for no reason. Cathleen thanked him and told him she would make sure the girl got the help she needed. She was glad the girl wouldn't have to be removed from her home. Cathleen and Aiden made small talk, but they were both busy and didn't spend much time on the phone. She figured he already knew Kevin and Kaitlin were coming in that weekend.

The next day, she made another trip out to the ranch. The mare was ready to foal, and Cathleen was glad she was there when it happened. Some of the kids were allowed to watch from afar if they didn't cause any distractions. The children were fascinated with Mother Nature. She enjoyed it as much as the kids. The ranch's stock was growing, and so was the business. The assistant told her the ranch was doing very well, and donations were still coming in for the help and upkeep. She loved to hear that families were also bringing their healthy children out to the ranch. She was thinking about providing a meal there once a day, with the kids participating in a talent show every Saturday. If Kaitlin chose to help out, she could be in charge of that. Maybe Bridget could make some cookies shaped like animals.

That Sunday was the day Kaitlin and Kevin were coming in. Cathleen and Bridget had time for church and lunch before picking Kaitlin up. Cathleen was sure Aiden and his aunt would be there for Kevin. The church sermon was about loving and forgiving one another. She was glad her family had all learned that by now. She didn't see Aiden at church, but when they stopped at a restaurant on the way to the airport, he was there with his aunt. When Cathleen and Bridget were invited over to their table, they made light, enjoyable conversation. She told Aiden and Fiona how both horse ranches were doing and how their families in Ireland were all pitching in to help. Aiden said he loved being back in New York. He said the people and lifestyle in California were very different from New York. He said he certainly hadn't left his heart there, which made them all laugh. She wondered if that statement had a double meaning. It would be awhile before she knew.

Chapter 23

The plane arrived on time, and Kevin and Kaitlin disembarked together. Apparently, they had caught up with each other before the plane left. Someone was nice enough to exchange a seat with one of them, and they chatted almost all the way. They had learned everything there was to know about their families by the time they arrived.

When they all reunited, Kevin was introduced to Bridget before he left with Aiden, and Kaitlin rode home with Cathleen and Bridget. Bridget said Kevin was a hottie and encouraged Cathleen to invite the O'Learys over to their apartment later that evening. It would be their only chance to get together again before the next workweek began.

When they all sat down together that evening, Aiden talked about his job at the hospital and how he loved working with the children he saw every day.

Kevin told of working for his dad at the gas company and how he needed a change and thought New York would be a great place to spend time with his little brother. Kevin was two inches shorter than his "little brother," but said he was a couple of years older and thus wiser.

Kaitlin said she had wanted to go to Hollywood but was scared to go alone. This left her second choice—and now she was in New York!

Aunt Fiona said she just wanted to retire and let someone else take care of her, but since there was no man in her life, that wasn't going to happen anytime soon.

Bridget said, "Well everyone knows what I do except Kevin, so I guess you will just have to come to the delicatessen and see for yourself."

"That I can do," said Kevin.

They all seemed to be having a good time reminiscing. Kevin said he would love to tour the ranch, and Aiden said he would schedule a day off. Cathleen told them to just let her know when they wanted to go to the ranch. She wanted to take Kaitlin soon, because she felt like she would love it. Bridget said she had first dibs on her and was going to use her in the deli. "Why can't she do both?" asked Cathleen.

Kaitlin spoke up. "Why doesn't anyone ask *me* what I want to do?" Both other women looked at her, and she said, "Why can't I do both?"

They laughed and said she could, but they would need to make a schedule to please everyone.

Kevin was enjoying himself by doing exactly as he pleased for the next few days—which meant walking around the city and enjoying the scenery and the different ethnic foods. He was able to get over to the delicatessen and visit Bridget one day, and they hit it off right away. She volunteered to take him out to the ranch on one of the slower days. She liked his sense of humor and felt like they would have a good time together. Since he didn't have much else to do, he hung out at the deli a lot and helped Bridget out in the office. He was good at getting things done. He had learned a lot from his father about managing a business.

It was slower in the middle of the week, so Bridget suggested they take a ride to the ranch. It took about an hour to get there, so they talked about their families. Bridget said she missed hers but planned on going to Ireland whenever her business got off the ground. She was blessed to have dependable employees she trusted.

Kevin said he really needed a break from the family business and had always wanted to come to the States. However, Aiden had beat him to it, so to speak. He therefore felt obligated to stay and help his dad. Business was good now, and he wasn't really needed there anymore.

Kevin was amazed to see how large the ranch was and how busy everyone was. It had even grown since Bridget's last visit. Kaitlin was in the process of rubbing down the horses and heard them drive up. She stepped out of the barn to speak to them and offered to show Kevin around. Bridget quickly informed her that would be her job since she was much more knowledgeable about this ranch than Kaitlin.

"I'll be performing later today, if you want to stay for the meal" Kaitlin replied.

"We just might do that" Bridget responded.

They had the food catered from a restaurant close by that gave them a discount. Bridget's business was too far away to think about catering anytime soon. Kaitlin played her banjo and sang an Irish ballad she had learned as a child while everyone enjoyed the meal.

A few children were there and wanted to participate. One child recited a poem, and two brothers sang a duet. Bridget had brought a few animal cookies, and gave them out to the children.

As Bridget and Kevin were getting ready to leave, they were both in a good mood. "We'll have to do this more often," said Kevin.

"They're always looking for volunteers," said Bridget, "but I like you helping me."

"Why can't I do both?" he said.

"You can. We don't want you foreigners getting bored over here," she said jokingly.

On their way out, they noticed that Aiden and Cathleen had just arrived

"Aiden had the afternoon off, so we thought it was the perfect time to come. If we knew you two were coming, we could have ridden together."

"I have to get back to work, but Kevin can stay if he wants to."

"Are you trying to get rid of me, lady?"

"No, I'm just saying…"

"Well, say it on the way back because I came with you and I'm going back with you."

"Okay, you two, you're sounding married already, and it's too soon for that!" Cathleen said. She was glad Kevin and Bridget were getting along so well.

Chapter 24

Aiden was impressed with what had been accomplished at the ranch in such a short time. He knew Geoffrey Henderson well and was assured that if anyone could make it work, he could.

Aiden wasn't used to riding, so Cathleen picked out a gentle mare for him and one of the stallions she had ridden before, for herself. She wanted to take a few children for a ride through the trails and asked Aiden if that was okay with him.

"Sure," he said, "I'll go with you."

They went to the stables to help get the horses saddled for the children riding the geldings. Cathleen rode with the children in front of her and Aiden in back. They rode the trails, mesmerized by the beautiful scenery below them. The trails, nestled among the pine trees, climbed higher and higher. The children were thrilled watching the squirrels jump from tree to tree and play with each other.

On the way back down, something spooked one of the geldings a child was riding, and it took off running. Cathleen yelled at the child to pull back on the reins, but he was too scared. As Cathleen chased after him, she was caught by a low hanging branch and thrown off her horse. The boy finally managed to rein in his horse and headed back to see what happened. Aiden had stopped the other kids and jumped off his horse to attend to Cathleen. She had passed out for a few seconds but was now moaning. Aiden had his cell phone so he called down to the office and told them what had happened, and gave them their location. He said he had already dialed 911, but told them to try and get an ambulance as close to them as possible. He said it looked like she had broken some bones and maybe fractured her ribs, as far as he could tell. He didn't want to move her, and suggested they get a gurney up to where they were. He asked one of the riders to come get the children and the horses, because he was staying with her. He was upset because of the carelessness of the maintenance team the ranch had hired and voiced his opinion.

"Get someone up here to clear up the branches hanging over the trail. This should *not* have happened!" He held Cathleen's hand and tried to calm her. She was worried, of course, about the safety of the kids.

"I made a mistake. I should have been the one in front to protect them," she said.

"I promise you that they are all fine. We have to get you to the hospital so they can diagnose your injuries.

"Do you know your full name?"

"Of course I do silly, it's Cathleen O'Connor.

"Do you know where you are right now?"

"Lying on the ground, looking up at you."

"Do you know the name of the president of the United States?"

Cathleen, in one of her rare moods said, "Yes, but I shouldn't have to tell you. It's George Herbert Walker Bush." Aiden knew then there was no head trauma.

When the pain became almost too much for Cathleen to bear, Aiden could only sit beside her and hold her hand. He prayed that she would be okay. He needed to remind her that he still loved her and wanted to marry her.

Thirty long minutes elapsed before he got a call that the ambulance had arrived at the ranch and was trying to get as close as they could so they could bring up the gurney. The trail was rugged, and there was an overgrowth of bushes alongside the path. Some of the tree branches had grown over the trail, which had caused Cathleen's fall.

Aiden heard the EMTs coming up the path and called out to them. Cathleen stirred when the men called her name. Aiden told them he had ruled out any brain trauma. She told them she hadn't hit her head, but it hurt to move, especially her shoulder and ribs. For precaution, they put a neck brace on her to stabilize her on the ride to the hospital. They gently put her on the gurney and started down the trail to the awaiting ambulance.

Aiden drove behind the ambulance and called Bridget to let her know what had happened. She and Kaitlin were waiting when the ambulance arrived at the hospital. The staff took her in for X-rays and discovered she had broken her collarbone and fractured several ribs. It was a miracle nothing else was broken, but she would still be out of commission for a while. She had surgery that afternoon, and since Aiden didn't want to leave her that night, he slept in the recliner in her room. When Cathleen woke up, she saw Aiden asleep in the recliner next to the bed. As she watched him lying there sleeping, she knew that she would never love another man as she did Aiden. No matter what happened between them, she was going to let him know.

Chapter 25

The breakfast tray arrived, and Aiden awoke to the sound of the knock on the door. He got up to help feed Cathleen, because every time she moved she was visibly in pain. She thanked the server and greeted Aiden. He immediately went into "doctor mode," wanting to know if she hurt anywhere and checking her bandages from the surgery. She wasn't used to him touching her body like that, but she realized that was what doctors did and complied. She let him help feed her and thanked him for being there for her.

"Where else did you think I would be? Haven't you gotten it through your head that I love you?"

"What about the girl you were engaged to? Didn't you love her too?"

"I tried to, but I couldn't forget you, so I came back to try one last time. Haven't you realized by now that I don't care if you have a disease or not? I don't want to spend another moment without you in my life."

Cathleen let out a sigh and said, "I know, and I don't either."

"I hope you don't have amnesia, and will remember what you just said."

"Do you want it in writing, Dr. O'Leary?"

He had been waiting so long to hear her say that, he hoped she really meant it.

"I don't want to go, but you will have plenty of friends coming by. Bridget will be here soon to stay with you, so rest, and I'll be back soon.

"Did you know she and Kevin were seeing each other now?"

"As in dating?"

"Yes."

"Well, I'm not surprised. I knew he was at the delicatessen a lot. I was worried about him getting bored, but I guess he found a way to entertain himself. They seem to fit each other well with their sense of humor."

Aiden left, and Bridget showed up about an hour later. She had to open the deli first and make sure things were running smoothly. Kevin offered to help out while she was gone.

Cathleen couldn't do much for herself, and they were keeping her pain-free, which meant she slept a lot. Aiden was back that night and went to talk to the doctor in charge before he went into her room. He explained how worried Cathleen was about getting the disease that seem to plague both her mothers. The doctor said that the disease running in her mother's family did not mean Cathleen would also inherit it. She had no symptoms, so they both agreed she was worrying for nothing. Aiden knew her fears of having to go through what her mothers had, had a lot to do with her reluctance to make some of her decisions. She was a strong woman, but even strong people break down when things overwhelm them.

He decided not to say anything until she was better. He wanted to marry her as soon as possible before she changed her mind. Since he knew God would work things out, he was leaving it in His hands.

Five days later, however, Cathleen was showing so much improvement the doctor thought she could go home and recover even faster. She was young, and her bones would heal quickly. She was happy to hear that, and so was Aiden. He knew he had to tell her what the doctor said, so he decided to tell her before she left the hospital. She needed to hear some good news for a change.

No one else was in the room. Aiden sat on the side of the bed and gave her the news. She had endured so much already, and now she had the man she loved, who was willing to take a chance on their happiness together. He explained again that it did not matter what was in the future; what mattered now was that she was okay. He loved her and wanted to marry her as soon as possible. He had not had time to purchase a ring but said, "Cathleen O'Connor, I would like to ask for your hand in marriage. I love you with all my heart and I will be the best husband and father I can be, and you will make me the happiest and luckiest man in the world if you say yes. I promise to have you a ring very soon."

Tears streamed down her face silently—not for herself, but for this wonderful man who loved her so very much.

"How could a woman turn down a proposal like that, especially looking like I do, and in a hospital bed to boot? So I had better say yes before you change your mind!"

They kissed for the first time in a long time, and it was the sweetest kiss from the sweetest man she had ever known. They heard clapping outside the door and realized some of the nurses and doctors had found out what was going on in room 237 and wanted to share in the happiness. Everyone wanted to know when and where the wedding would be, and whether they were invited.

Six weeks later, Aiden and Cathleen were planning the wedding—which would be, of course, at the ranch. It seemed so appropriate to Cathleen, and Aiden agreed only because it meant so much to her. Bridget, Kaitlin, and Cathleen went shopping for the perfect dresses but had unanimously decided to keep things simple.

Bridget was going to cater the event, in spite of the distance. Some of the relatives from Ireland were coming. Cathleen couldn't remember when she had ever been this happy. She chose April 15 because it was Grandfather Charlie's birthday. It was because of him that she had found her birth mother. She told Aiden about the Claddagh ring her grandfather had given her and explained the significance of the ring, which was produced in the seventeenth century. She then asked if he would mind giving her that ring at their wedding

Chapter 26

Bridget helped Cathleen plan the wedding, and everything went off without a hitch. They decided on a traditional wedding, and the priest complied. The families all got along well, and they couldn't have asked for a more perfect day. Cathleen wanted her and Aiden to come riding in on a horse, but that was overruled—though he did consent to them coming in a horse-drawn buggy. They decided to have it in the big recreation room where they ate and had their weekly talent shows. Since it was outside the city, they found a local priest to marry them, and they wrote their own vows.

As they held hands, Cathleen spoke first. "Since the first day I met you at the sandwich shop, I knew there was something special about you. You were always present even when I was not—and so secure about your love for me when I was scared to commit. You hung in there while I was teetering and unsure of myself. It took an accident to wake me up and realize I could never find another man like you, nor would I want to. Aiden O'Connor, if you will have me as your wife, I promise to love and cherish you from this moment on and never forget to tell you what a wonderful husband you are. I may not always obey you, but I'll always love you!"

Aiden said, "I will." The audience laughed.

Then Aiden spoke. "Cathleen, I can't even imagine my life without you. You have been my fair-haired beauty since the first day you spoke my name. You captured my heart then, and there has never been another I could love as I love you. It took an accident to knock some sense into that pretty head of yours. This ring is a symbol of our love and represents friendship, love, and loyalty. If you will accept my hand in marriage, I promise to love you, cherish you, and honor you the rest of my days."

Cathleen said, "I will."

The couple exchanged rings, and the priest read from the Bible.

"Well, I don't think anyone here will oppose this wedding, but if there is one, you may speak now or forever hold your peace." As no one did, the priest said, "There's not much more to be said except I pronounce you husband and wife. You may kiss your bride."

At the end of the ceremony, as they walked out, a butterfly landed on Cathleen's shoulder. Aiden noticed it first and pointed it out to her. "That's a sign of good luck," he said. *We're going to need more than good luck*, she thought to herself.

They had discussed where they wanted to go on their honeymoon, and since most of their relatives had come over for the wedding, there was no need to go to Ireland. So the next best place to go without leaving the States was Hawaii. Aiden had made the reservations with a cruise line to go for a week. They flew over and went on the ship the following day.

Ten days later, they were back at their jobs. Aiden was finishing up his internship, and Cathleen was back at her desk in her office at the food bank. Things were going very well for Geoffrey and

Maria, and she wondered about the possibility of another wedding on the horizon. Bridget wasn't ready to settle down, but Kevin wasn't letting her too far out of his sight. Kaitlin was happy just being Kaitlin. Singing was her passion, and she hoped to make it in the music world one day. In the meantime Cathleen had moved into Aiden's nice condo and let the girls take over her place.

Cathleen started to notice she was tired a lot and needed more rest, just like her mother when she first began to get sick. She noticed some occasional dizziness, and assumed the disease was approaching. She hadn't said anything to Aiden, but he was a doctor and noticed her apprehension. They never spoke about it. Aiden prayed that it wasn't the disease she thought it was, and Cathleen prayed that she would not be a burden on her family. Cathleen was still able to drive and do her social work.

She noticed she was sleeping a lot and started having nausea in the mornings. She didn't think the nausea was from an autoimmune disease, so out of curiosity she bought a pregnancy test and discovered why. She was so happy she called Aiden at work to let him know. He insisted she go to the doctor soon to be checked, so she made an appointment with a friend who was an obstetrician. She was only two and a half months along, but the doctor gave her strict orders to follow. He told her that her blood pressure was low, and that would cause the dizziness. He said to watch for signs of loss of coordination or balance, because she had to be careful not to fall. She promised to be careful. She knew she would have to use a walker if she started losing her balance.

Aiden would drop her off at work every day, and if he was going to be very late, someone would bring her home. She didn't like having to depend on people but knew she had no other choice. Besides, it was a blessing that she had such a loving circle of friends and family. Aunt Fiona (she could call her that now) would come over on the weekends and help her get the chores done. She was getting more tired as she got further along in the pregnancy and found it harder to get up in the mornings and get moving. She decided to cut back on her workload and do her paperwork from home.

She slept in after Aiden had left for work and finally got up around noon. She went into the kitchen to get some juice. When she opened the refrigerator to pick up the bottle of juice, she lost her grip on the bottle, and it fell to the floor, juice spilling everywhere. Cathleen started to fall and reached for the chair to stay upright. She felt hands around her waist and was gently placed on a chair. She looked around to see who was there, but of course there was no one there but her—or was there? She wasn't sure anyone would believe her if she told them. She gave a prayer of thanks.

At her next appointment, she told the doctor of her near mishap but didn't mention what happened because he would think she was delusional. He examined her and said she was a lucky girl this time. He suggested that she start thinking about using a walker now before something bad happened. She thought it was unnecessary but didn't want to take any chances on falling. She told Aiden she had almost fallen, but didn't go into detail. Every morning after that, there was juice beside her bed. Aiden brought home a walker with a seat so she could wheel herself around and sit down if she needed to. She was growing in size every week and knew the time was getting near.

Chapter 27

S he called his name softly. "Aiden, I think it's time." He was snoring away and didn't hear her; he was such a sound sleeper. She nudged him with a little pressure, and that got his attention. He sat up in bed this time and said, "Is it time?"

"Yes, dear, it's time for Baby O'Leary to greet the world."

She already had her bags packed, and Aiden jumped up, got dressed, and called the hospital to let them know they were coming.

A nurse was waiting for them with a wheelchair when they got to the emergency room. They arrived at 3:30 a.m., and Baby O'Leary was born on April 15 at 7:37 a.m., a year to the date after their wedding! It was a baby boy, and Aiden was able to be in the delivery room. The doctor let him cut the umbilical cord, and he was the first to hold the baby. When the nurse had cleaned him up, she handed him to his mother. At least this time the reason they were in the hospital was joyful, and Cathleen was overjoyed to have a baby who looked so much like his father. He had a head of brownish-red hair and bright blue eyes. They took the baby to the nursery and wheeled Cathleen to her room close by. She encouraged Aiden to go on to work. She said she would be just fine. He didn't want to leave but knew she would have a lot of friends and family popping in to see her and the baby. He kissed her and said he would be back later.

Bridget left Kevin in charge of the deli and she called before leaving for the hospital to let her family and friends know the good news. It was like a reunion when everyone arrived. Bridget had to call a halt when she saw Cathleen was getting tired, so they let her rest. Aunt Fiona dropped by at noon. She had been volunteering at the food bank and said Maria and Geoffrey would be by later.

The girls had been planning a baby shower but had put it off until they knew the sex. Now they could go ahead and have one after Cathleen got home. All she had to do was relax and open the baby's gifts. She wanted to breast-feed, but after careful consideration, she changed her mind. Aunt Fiona bought baby bottles and formula. The baby had more clothes than he needed, but most everyone was smart enough to buy some bigger sizes for the future. The guys even showed up too but went to the game room to play pool and watch television while the women did their thing.

Everyone chipped in to help clean up before leaving. Fiona got the baby clothes ready to wash, dry, and put away in the baby's room. Bridget and Kaitlin had decorated the room with birds, bugs, and butterflies—perfect for a little boy's room and something he could grow into, with a baby bed that turned into a youth bed.

Cathleen started taking pictures of baby O'Leary right away to send over to Ireland. As her mind drifted back to when she had gone there for the first time, she wished her son could have known his great-grandfather Charlie. She knew her grandfather had raised a wonderful son who had taken care of her mother 'til the end. She regretted that it had taken so long for both sides of the family to know each other. She didn't know how long she would have on this earth but hoped their child would get to know his relatives from Ireland.

When Aiden came home that evening, he noticed a change in Cathleen. There seemed to be contentment about her he had never seen before. He asked her if everything was okay, and she replied, "Yes, everything is perfect, my love." That night, as they lay in bed, Cathleen said, "I was thinking today, since we haven't filled out the birth certificate yet, that I would like to call him Charles Murphy O'Leary. Grandfather Charlie was born on April 15. We married on April 15, and our baby was born on April 15. Doesn't that sound like a good reason to name him that? When I talked to Grandfather Charlie, he told me to find my real mother, which I did, and for us to be happy, which we are."

"Yes, we are dear. Can we go to sleep now before little Charlie wakes up for another bottle?"

Chapter 28

Cathleen had stayed home for three months now, but was getting antsy to get back to work. Her health seemed to have improved immensely after the birth of little Charlie. She had been throwing little hints around when Aiden was home. Finally, one day he suggested to her that maybe Aunt Fiona might be available a few days a week to watch the baby so Cathleen could ride to the office with him, depending on how well she felt. He knew she missed her work, and Charlie was still so young for her to take to the office, even though he would get lots of attention there.

Aunt Fiona said she would love to care for him now that she was retired. Now Cathleen just needed to make sure she could do all the things she needed to do on her own. Her tiredness seemed to have improved, but she always took precautions with Charlie.

Aiden suggested she make an appointment with her doctor before deciding to go back. So Cathleen made the appointment. Aunt Fiona took her and sat with Charlie in the waiting room. Her examination went well, and the doctor was surprised at how well she was doing. He told Cathleen he could see no reason why she couldn't go back to work as long as she felt up to it. He told her to let him know if there were any changes. He could put her on medications for dizziness if she started having symptoms again.

Everyone was happy to see her back at the office. The food bank volunteers would pop in and out during the day, asking about little Charlie and when she would be bringing him in. She told them soon. His little personality was starting to blossom, and she could see he was going to be a happy baby. She always prayed that he had his father's genes and personality. Aiden was always an upbeat and positive person about everything, and she hoped he passed it along to his son. He certainly looked like him, so she knew he would be a charmer.

Maria's law practice was taking off, and she was eager to have Cathleen back at her office. She and Geoffrey were still dating; however, there were no plans for marriage yet. Geoffrey was much more established now, and being a few years older than Maria, he would have loved to tie the knot, but knew Maria was not in the same place right now. Neither was interested in anyone else, and he sure wasn't going anywhere. They were both happy to see Cathleen back at her desk. She had a couple of cases pending and needed Maria's advice on them. Bridget popped in at noon and brought lunch for everyone. Cathleen still had a few pounds to lose, but she could not resist her cousin's good food. When Aiden called and found out Bridget had brought lunch over, he said, "Save some for me. I'll be right over!" He was only about ten minutes from the food bank and never turned down an opportunity to have some of Bridget's Irish food.

Kevin was still helping out at the ranch when they needed him. He was a lot like his brother in his work ethic. Bridget liked being around him because they had such fun together. They made such a cute couple, and it was good to see the two together. They seemed to be serious about each other, although marriage was never mentioned.

Kaitlin helped at the delicatessen whenever she could, but she stayed busy at the ranch while trying to pursue a music career. She always took the time to call and check on everyone. She had written another song and mailed it in to one of the recording studios, hoping to get recognized for her talent one day. She loved working at the ranch and the deli, but neither job fulfilled her lifelong dreams.

Cathleen realized she would have to pace herself if she wanted to continue working, so she made a list of projects to take on every day. If she couldn't get them all done, she would just add what was left to the next day's list. Her main project right now was Charlie, and she wanted to have some energy left for him when she got home. Aunt Fiona was so good to them and suggested that she and Aiden have a night out every so often while she watched Charlie. She offered to keep him overnight, but Cathleen couldn't stand the thought of not waking up to him every morning.

When Aiden had a Saturday off, they would all three go to the park together. The same vendor was there who had sold them hot dogs several years ago, and he remembered them. He had even taken his daughter in to see Aiden for her first checkup.

"Do you remember what we talked about when we came here?" asked Cathleen.

"Yes, I certainly do, my love. You needed to tell me about Darcy being your real mother, not Margaret, and you were having trouble dealing with all of this so suddenly in your young life. I told you then I would always be here for you. Look where we are today! I'm back on the same bench with you and loving you more with each passing day!"

"Thank you for being so patient with me and giving me the time I needed to sort things out. What a wonderful family we have now. Because of God's blessing, we have a beautiful baby boy."

Chapter 29

C athleen was taking the day off and decided to go through some of the files in her desk at home. She noticed the journal she had started before Charlie was born. It had been a while since she had written in it, and she needed to catch up. She opened it up to review what she had written:

November 1992

Good morning, baby O'Leary,

I am so glad to have you in my tummy, and so is Daddy. I know you will be a beautiful girl or boy. Whichever God chooses for us, I know you will be a blessing. You have been with us for four months now, and I can feel you moving around. Maybe you are just stretching or trying to get comfortable. Just hang in there for another five months and we will meet each other face to face.

We love you already my little angel!

Mommy

March 1993

Another four months have gone by, and I must say you are a rambunctious little one. Sometimes I lie awake at night with my hand on my stomach, and it feels like you are playing a game—maybe basketball, like your dad used to play when he had the time. I am glad you are active, for that makes me feel like you are healthy. I have lots to tell you one day when you are older and can understand better. Sometimes I wish you could stay right here in my tummy where it's nice and safe and warm, but that is not God's plan. Besides, then we couldn't hold you or play with you and tell you how much we love you. God had a plan for us all along, and His plan is always perfect. I'll try to sleep a while now while you are resting.

Loving you already!

Mommy

My precious little one, I almost fell today because I wasn't as careful as I should have been—but God was merciful, and no harm has come to either of us. It would have broken my heart if I had harmed you, so I am being more careful now until I can hold you in my arms.

Always loving you,
Mommy

April 1993

My darling baby boy,

 A week ago today was the fifteenth, and your big day finally came. Off to the hospital we went. You are now considered a tax deduction! I will explain that to you one day. We decided to name you after my grandfather on my daddy's side, and your middle name is after my mother's side—so now you are officially Charles Murphy O'Leary! You have very good lungs, so maybe you will be a singer like your cousin Kaitlin. Your daddy got to cut the cord (I will explain that later) and hold you before I did. I was happy to be next in line. I am very tired now, so maybe we can both sleep.

Loving you always,
Mommy

July 1993

My precious Charlie,

 Your great Aunt Fiona has graciously agreed to take care of you while I work a few days a week. She will take good care of you and sing you Irish lullabies. I will miss every minute we're not together, but I will soon be able to bring you to work with me. You will get so spoiled by all the attention you will get, but we will love you anyway! I am home today and get to watch you play in your crib while I do paperwork. You remind me of your dad when you are sleeping. What sweet faces you both have!

Loving you always,
Mommy

Cathleen put the journal and pen back in the drawer and got up to get Charlie's bottle ready; then they could both rest before Aiden came home. She had prepared a casserole earlier, so dinner was ready to be heated. Charlie woke her up fussing about an hour later, so she got up, patted him, and changed his diaper. As she went to lie back down, she noticed she was dizzy. *I'm just tired*, she thought, lying back down. When she woke back up, the dizziness was gone, so she thought no more of it. If it came back, she'd let the doctor know. She would have to learn to pace herself better now that she was a mommy. She loved that word and couldn't wait to hear Charlie say it. Of course, it may be *daddy* first, but she never minded being second with these two.

Chapter 30

Nine months later, Charlie had his first birthday. There were balloons in the front yard with a big sign that read Happy First Birthday, Charlie. Everyone from Aiden's clinic and all the food bank volunteers were invited, along with their families. It was a very festive event with more toys than Charlie could ever play with. They would donate most of them to the Family Crisis Center. Charlie enjoyed just playing with the paper and boxes they came in. Bridget baked his cake, and it was filled with a special Irish cream with chocolate and vanilla layers. It had a big number one candle on it. Everyone sang "Happy Birthday" to him while he sat in his high chair. He tried to sing along with them and clapped his little icing-smeared hands, which brought lots of laughter. Apparently, Aunt Fiona had been singing around him since he was born, and he was pretty good for a one-year-old, even if he didn't always get the words right. That made it more enjoyable!

Many pictures were taken for the photo album, and more memories were made. Bridget and Kaitlin hung around and cleaned up. Cathleen and Charlie disappeared to the bedroom for some quiet time. Aiden retrieved a big box from the garage for the toys that would be given away.

Aiden found Cathleen rocking Charlie, and they were both almost asleep as he entered the room. Aiden picked Charlie up and placed him in his crib. He was growing fast and would have to go into his youth bed before much longer. Cathleen smiled as she watched Aiden take on the role of fatherhood. She was glad he had chosen pediatrics as his profession. There was nothing like having a doctor living in your home! She would never have believed she could be this happy again.

Time seemed to fly by. The ranches in New Jersey and Ireland seem to be doing wonders for the people going there. Her grandfather's lawyer kept her informed about the Ireland ranch, so she didn't have to fly back now. She couldn't have asked for a better management team there or in the States. She wasn't sure how much longer she could hold onto Kaitlin; the girl had a briar in her britches and was itching to get it out. She had not heard from anyone about her songs, but that was not stopping her. She had gotten a band together, and when she wasn't at the ranch, she was playing anywhere that would pay her. When she came around, she would sit with Charlie on her lap, play the guitar, and sing. Charlie would try to help her out by singing with her. He knew a lot of the words to her songs now. She told him one day they were going to sing a duet together, and he said, "Okay, Katy!" and gave her a high five.

Cathleen started reading Bible stories to Charlie at night. He especially liked the one of baby Moses placed in a basket in the Nile. He loved being read to and would always ask a lot of questions that Cathleen answered as best she could to a small child going on three. He never seemed to get tired of hearing those stories and would say, "Read me more, Mommy!"

"I will tomorrow night, okay, my little buddy?" Cathleen would say.

And he would always say, "Okay, Mommy."

Before Cathleen left him for the night, they would say their prayers together.

Chapter 31

Cathleen hadn't been feeling very well lately and couldn't seem to get enough sleep. The nausea had returned, and she couldn't believe she might be pregnant again. When Aiden heard her retching in the bathroom one morning, he made her an appointment with a doctor in his office building. He told Aiden he would work her in. He then called Aunt Fiona to see if they could bring Charlie by. That day, they found out that Cathleen was indeed pregnant.

Charlie loved going to see his great-aunt because there was a playground nearby that she would take him to. He wasn't a bashful boy and loved playing with the other kids. He was almost three now and was so excited to learn he would have a brother or sister. He didn't understand why they didn't know if it was going to be a boy or girl, so Cathleen left that up to his Dad to explain. They didn't want any surprises this time, so they would find out the baby's sex during a sonogram. Not wanting to take any chances on falling, she would be much more careful this time around. Charlie was such a good boy and let her sleep in in the mornings. He was good at entertaining himself and sang as he played. Sometimes he would line up his stuffed animals, tell Bible stories, and sing to them. She would hear him singing songs she had never heard before, so she thought he might become a writer as well.

Cathleen thought she was gaining weight fast, but it was becoming more and more difficult to turn down all the good food everybody brought her. She and Aiden had gone for the sonogram and found out it was a girl this time. Now they could choose a name for the baby. Cathleen wanted a name starting with a C, and they agreed on Charleen. The first part of her name was pronounced Char, like in Charlie, and the last part of her name was pronounced like the last part of Cathleen's name, so she would be named after her grandfather and her mother. They asked Charlie what he thought of the name, and he said, "Okay, I like Charleen. When is she coming home?" This called for another lesson in Mother Nature, so she let him feel the baby moving in her tummy. All he could say was "Wow, that's cool, Mommy." It became a ritual every day for him to feel baby Charleen, and when he would ask when the baby was coming out, Cathleen would say, "Soon, Charlie. Soon."

She realized she should have already started a journal on her baby girl. She had bought a journal the last time she and Bridget had gone shopping but had been preoccupied and forgotten about it. She got up to look for the book, and it was still in the bag on the shelf where she'd left it. She carefully pulled it down and reached for a pen. She put Charlie in the playpen on the porch, sat in her lounge chair, and started writing:

> *Hello, my darling baby girl,*
> *How wonderful those words are to your daddy and me.*
> *You have a big brother, and we are all waiting patiently for*

you to arrive. Some days I wish you were already here, but I know it is not time yet, so we will have to wait. It seems you are going to be a big girl, because I have gained so much weight. Maybe I'm just trying to eat for the both of us when I know I don't have to. You are going to be so pretty in all your new clothes Aunt Bridget and I bought for you. I will show you off to everyone at church, and they will love you as much as we do.

Loving you always,

Mommy

As Cathleen sat there writing, she began to get drowsy, laid the pen and book down, and drifted off. She was startled awake when Charlie called her name, saying, "I'm hungry Mommy."

"Okay, Charlie, let's go get something to eat, sweetheart." She was glad Charlie had been in his playpen when she fell asleep. He must have taken a nap too, for they had been on the porch a couple of hours. She had to be more careful in the future.

Cathleen's water broke in the middle of the night, and she was prepared this time. It wasn't so hard to get Aiden up this time. He notified the hospital like before, and within fifteen minutes they had gotten dressed, readied her bag, put Charlie in the car, and notified the hospital.

This birth was a little more difficult than the last one. Cathleen had gained a lot of fluid with her weight gain, and Charleen wasn't ready to come out of her warm safety nest yet. She finally arrived on September 12. She didn't cry right away, but one tap on her behind changed all that! She was a beautiful baby with blonde curly hair like her mom—but she wasn't as big a baby as Cathleen had thought. It was all that fluid she carried that made her feel fat!

No one had been able to come from Ireland, but Cathleen would send pictures soon. A week later, she wrote in her journal:

> *My precious Charleen,*
>
> *You finally made it into the world, baby girl, and we couldn't be happier to finally meet you. You have my curly blonde hair and remind me so much of your grandmother Darcy, who is in heaven now. You are such a good baby, and you sleep more than your brother did at your age. He's been such a good big brother to you. He helped to feed and rock you your first week here on earth. He sang to you and you made faces at him, but it could have been gas pains—I hope it wasn't his singing! Maybe you two will sing together one day. I love you more than words can say.*
>
> > *Loving you always,*
> > *Mommy*

Chapter 32

Charleen was a good baby. She hardly ever cried—the opposite of Charlie at that age. At her six month visit, the doctor listened to her heart a little longer than usual and said he thought he heard a faint heart murmur and that they would need to keep close watch on it. Sometimes murmurs closed on their own, he said, and if not, they could do surgery when she got older. When Cathleen expressed concern to Aiden, he said, "The doctor will keep close watch on her. She's still a baby, and the murmur may heal on its own—but you can't expect her to be as active as Charlie." She thought she might be worried about something that wouldn't materialize, but that was what mothers did.

Cathleen took a leave of absence to be home with Charleen. She seemed to be doing fine. She just slept more than usual, and she was such a good baby. Cathleen had plenty of help spoiling and holding her. Charleen also loved being sung to, and she got her share of Irish lullabies from her cousins Bridget, Kaitlin, and Great-Aunt Fiona.

It didn't seem like she should be one year old next week, and Cathleen would be taking Charleen back for another physical soon. They decided not to have a birthday party for her, but Bridget made her a big cupcake with a number one candle on it. Only the family came this time, and they managed to get cute pictures of her with a cupcake face trying to blow the candle out. Then they all jumped in to help her open her presents. Pictures were sent to family in Ireland.

There had been no changes in Charleen's heart until the doctor examined her at age three. He told her parents the hole in her heart was not closing, and since tests showed that it had actually gotten bigger, the doctor scheduled surgery for the next morning. They admitted Charleen that night, and her mom stayed with her while Aiden went home with Charlie. He would take Charlie over to Aunt Fiona's in the morning. The next morning, Charleen was prepared for surgery, and Cathleen stayed with her as long as possible. Then she went to the chapel to pray for her little girl. Aiden kept her informed throughout the surgery, and after it was over and they learned that everything had gone well, Cathleen went to stay by her side. The nurses brought her a tray of food so she wouldn't have to leave. Her family offered to stay with her, but Cathleen would not leave. They kept Charleen comfortable, and when she came to, she said, "Hi, Mommy, I've been gone bye-bye, but I'm back now."

"Yes, you are my angel. Welcome back."

"Where did I go, Mommy? You weren't there."

"But I'm here now, baby, and I'm not going anywhere."

Cathleen was able to bring Charleen home after a week. Charlie was so happy to see his baby sister and have her back home again. His mom told him he had to handle his little sister very carefully since she had a boo-boo in her chest. He was so sweet with her and wanted to rock her, so Cathleen let him sit with them in the rocker.

Charlie was six now and would be starting first grade soon. He would be going to a private Catholic school and would be wearing a uniform every day, which made things easier for Cathleen. The bus would pick him up right outside their condo. Cathleen and Aiden had visited the school with Charlie, and met his teacher so they would feel comfortable on his first day. Aiden recognized his teacher, because she had brought her son, Randy, in for his physical last year. Charlie and Randy would become good friends over the years. They were good boys, for the most part, but did get in a jam when he and Randy stopped to watch a group of older boys playing basketball. Charlie missed his bus, and Randy's mom had to bring Charlie home. Cathleen made him pinky swear to never do that again!

Cathleen had gone back to work at the office part time again while Aunt Fiona cared for Charleen. On the weekends when Aiden had time off, the family would pick up Randy and go to the ranch for a ride. Aiden didn't want Cathleen to ride anymore, so she led Charleen around on one of the ponies, leaving Aiden to ride with the boys. He had been riding more and felt at ease on a saddle now. The maintenance crew was keeping the trails free of overgrown brush and overhanging tree branches now, thanks to Aiden.

Chapter 33

Over the years, Cathleen's dizziness and tiredness had come back, and after lab work, the doctor put her on iron pills for anemia. She hadn't been having the recurring dreams, or if she did, she didn't remember them.

Aiden noticed Cathleen was having more headaches. She had a doctor's appointment the following week, and he asked Aunt Fiona to take her. The doctor told her it was time to go on medication to try and keep her headaches under control. She agreed, and they got the prescription filled before heading home. Her stubbornness and will to live had kept her around so far. God had been very gracious to her, and she never failed to thank Him for her blessings.

They got home just as Charlie arrived. He asked if he could go down to the gym in the condo and practice some hoops. Aunt Fiona said she would love to watch him before she went home. He changed clothes and had a snack before heading down. Fiona urged Cathleen to go with them. She could take her walker with her, and Fiona and Charleen could sit on the benches. A few guys were there practicing too, and they let Charlie join in. He was getting tall, and was agile like his dad. Cathleen had seen a growth spurt over the summer. He was very good at his game, and the men were amazed at his ability to hit the goal every time.

As Aunt Fiona told them good-bye, they went back to their suite. Cathleen took the walker to the bedroom and walked out to sit in her chair. She almost made it to the chair before she lost her balance. Charlie saw what happened and rushed to her side.

"Don't worry, Mom. I'm here. I won't let you fall."

"I know you won't, Charlie. I just hate that you have to see me this way."

Time seemed to fly by, and Charlie was in high school now and doing very well. He was a gifted student and had inherited his father's love of sports. He was able to go to Abraham Lincoln High, where his mom and dad had attended. Charleen was eleven now and loved spending time with her brother. She wasn't into sports like Charlie, but she had inherited the love of singing and had started drawing when she was in first grade. She was so talented that her teachers encouraged her to take art classes, which were scheduled three times a week. Her bedroom walls were covered with her creations! She loved to go outside to find a good spot to sit and draw scenery. Cathleen wondered more than once where this talent had come from. She didn't know enough about her Irish background to even speculate about it. She was rather sure it hadn't come from her parents, because she had seen no evidence of such growing up. Aiden never had time, and she couldn't draw a straight line. Charleen had the quiet nature of her mother and grandmother Darcy, and seemed content to sit and draw for hours on end. Cathleen was so thankful her heart murmur had been repaired and that she was as healthy as any other eleven-year-old.

Kaitlin finally got a hit record and moved to Las Vegas to sing at one of the clubs there. She still came back when she could, and she and Charlie would sing together at the ranch. His parents didn't know it, but he had been singing in the band with her before she left for Vegas. Charleen overheard him talking about it, but she promised not to tell. His parents thought he was off playing ball with his friends. He hadn't really lied to them; he would just say he was going off with his friends, which he did. He had been singing since he could walk—it just came naturally. Kaitlin could play any instrument and had taught Charlie to play the guitar. They had written a song together and planned to surprise his parents with it one day when the time was right.

Chapter 34

When Charlie and Charleen came home from school one afternoon, his mom asked them to sit with her awhile. She had been thinking about what they should know about her family, and she believed honesty was the best policy. They would find out eventually, and she wanted it to come from her. Just then, the phone rang, and their talk was put off for another time. The call was from her aunt Clara. Her grandparents were up in their years now and had been put in a nursing facility. Grandpa Quilan had Alzheimer's, had fallen, and was now unconscious, and Grandma Deidre had had a heart attack. Now both were in the hospital. Clara said it didn't look good for either of them, so they needed to think about coming back soon. Cathleen said she would let the family know.

She didn't expect Bridget or Kevin to go, because they had family there to represent them. Charlie and Charleen were excited about going to Ireland. Aiden was the only one having to take emergency leave. He thankfully found a doctor who could take his patients. They were able to get a flight out the following day.

Grandpa Quinlan died the day they arrived. He wouldn't have known any of them anyway, so maybe it was a blessing that the children would not see him like that. Grandma Deidre was still hanging on, but when she found out her husband had passed, she had no desire to linger on in this world and said she wanted to go on to be with her husband. She asked for no other medication to be administered to her, and they complied with her wishes. She was happy to see her granddaughters, Kaitlin and Cathleen, and to see her great-grandson and great-granddaughter for the first time in person.

As everyone left the room, Deidre asked Cathleen if she could stay for a few minutes. Cathleen took her hand and asked her grandmother what was on her mind. She said, "I have pondered over whether I should tell you this for years now, but I have kept it long enough. You may do with this information what you wish." She then told her granddaughter that her mother Darcy had become engaged to an American shortly after coming back from New York, and after they married, she became pregnant. The thought of what she had done with Daniel and of the baby she'd already given away overwhelmed her. She became depressed and refused to see her husband. The birth of her second child was a difficult one, and she went into seclusion. Deidre called Jeremy and told him he had a baby girl, and that was when he found out Darcy had had a nervous breakdown. Deidre had been taking care of Darcy and the baby, and it was just too much for her. Deidre told him Darcy wasn't able to take care of herself now, let alone a baby, and she was too old to be raising another child. That was when Jeremy decided to go back to the States with the baby and raise her.

Losing both babies was just too much for Darcy to bear, and when she could stand it no longer, she tried to take her own life.

Cathleen wondered why Darcy had never told her about her half-sister. She was glad Darcy had survived her suicide attempt, or she would never have gotten to know and love her. She would now look for the half-sister she had never known she had.

"No one ever spoke of her pregnancy again, and Darcy never tried to contact Jeremy. She felt she wasn't deserving of another child, and she had never really gotten over Daniel. She would be about four years younger than you. I was never told what she was named, but I know the father's name. I have kept this information all these years. I want you to have it now." Deidre took the paper from her Bible and handed it to Cathleen. She kissed her grandmother and thanked her for telling her.

Still in shock, Cathleen met up with her family in the lobby. She wasn't sure what, if anything, to do, so she kept the information to herself. Later that evening, they all returned to the hospital. Deidre was very weak but told them she would love for the family to come and sing an Irish lullaby to her one more time. The hospital granted her wish. The family filled up the room and circled her bed. They all held hands and sang to her one last time. You could hear the singing from her room throughout the cardiology floor. There wasn't a dry eye in the room when they finished. They took turns kissing her good-bye. They felt she would be with Grandpa Quinlan before the day was done. She died peacefully with a smile on her face two hours later, a teardrop still on her cheek.

Funeral services were held at the same Catholic church as Grandfather Charlie's and her mom's, with the same priest presiding. Charlie and Charleen finally were able to meet their great-grandmother Myrna and the relatives that were left.

Grandma Deidre and Grandpa Quinlan were buried together on the same day. It simply made sense to do it that way.

While they were there, the family went by to see the ranch. It had become a very popular place for all kids, and Cathleen could not be happier with the ranch's progress. Later that day Cathleen took her children down to the trail behind the Murphys' house that led to the stream where her mother had died. She told them her mom and dad would meet there when they were young but did not go into any other details. She would tell them both that story at another time and place.

Five days later, they were back at home. It had been a fast and sad five days, but Cathleen knew her grandparents were ready to go, and the Lord did too. They went to church on Sunday and lit a candle for the family.

Chapter 35

Cathleen didn't go into work as often now. Maria said she would call her if they needed to discuss a case. One afternoon Cathleen decided to call Maria and ask her if she could come in to discuss a private matter with her. Maria told her to ride in with Aiden when she felt like it and that she would make time for her. She hadn't told Aiden about her grandmother's revelation yet. She wasn't sure if she would be able to find her half-sister's father or where he would be after all these years. She wanted more information before telling her family anything. She was able to see Maria the next day and gave her the only information she had. Maria knew a private investigator who owed her a favor. She said she would turn the information over to him and ask him to see what he could find out.

Charlie was a senior now. He was as healthy as any teenager, and playing sports had kept him fit. Cathleen didn't know where the time had gone. Charlie was seventeen, and Charleen was fourteen. It was hard to believe Charlie was graduating. Where had her babies gone? She knew she had to tell them both about her mothers and their accidents. She felt it was her obligation to let them know. She felt Charleen was mature enough to understand, and Cathleen didn't want to put it off any longer. One afternoon she was feeling rather good and decided to make this the day. When they came home from school, Charlie was ready to go out to meet his friends. His mother called him and Charleen to her side.

"If you will sit down with me, I would like to tell you a little story about my younger days. I think it's time you both know the truth about my family."

They were both intrigued as they sat down on the sofa. She told them about how she had started to help take care of her mom when she was ten. Their dad had already told them a few details about how their grandfather Daniel and grandmother Margaret had come over from Ireland and about the fire. However, they didn't know that Margaret wasn't Cathleen's birth mom. She told them about finding her biological mom in Ireland and how she had helped take care of them both until the accidents.

Cathleen said she had taken them both down to the stream behind her grandparents' house for two reasons. One was because her dad had met her mom down there. The other was that she often took her biological mother there when she was taking care of her—and that was where she'd had her accident and drowned. Cathleen wasn't ready to mention the discovery of a half-sister in the family yet, because she had not heard anything from Maria yet.

Charlie and Charleen sat there taking it all in, realizing now all that their mother had gone through and why she was so concerned about the disease. They told her, "We're here now, Mom, and we won't let anything happen to you—not while we're around."

"We don't know if the autoimmune gene runs in the family or not, and I pray that the gene skipped you two. You know heart disease runs on your great-grandfather Charlie's side of the family also, but Charleen's heart has been fixed."

Charlie told his mom he had been checked out all of his life by his dad and was in great physical shape. "I don't want to worry about something I don't know will happen anyway. I have my education to concentrate on right now."

"Now may I please go?"

Cathleen laughed and said, "Yes, please go!" Charleen stayed with her mom and told her she wasn't worried about any genes right now. She liked her genes just fine. As Cathleen was sitting with her daughter, she realized neither of them was worried about their future, and that made her very happy. She prayed her children took after their father's family. It gave her comfort to know they were at ease about what she had told them.

Chapter 36

The O'Leary family finally moved into their very own ranch-style home outside of the city. Several acres of land surrounded the house, and Cathleen loved taking her walker and walking around the yard, taking in the beautiful scenery. There was no stream nearby, just beautiful trees, wild flowers, and the smell of fresh air. What else could anyone want?

Senior pictures had come back, and if she didn't know they were of Charlie, she would have thought it was Aiden. They had done a good job raising him, although sometimes it takes a village. She was so grateful to have such wonderful family and friends. Next week, Charlie would be graduating from Abraham Lincoln. They had been able to keep him in the same school since it was his last year.

It was still hard for Cathleen to believe all that had taken place in the last forty-one years. She didn't expect anyone from Ireland to come over for the graduation, but she knew there would be plenty of family and friends present. She couldn't help but remember Darcy and Bridget showing up at her own graduation and making a spectacle of themselves by standing up and shouting her name.

Bridget and Kevin had met up previously with Kaitlin in Las Vegas. They were married in a little chapel there, with Kaitlin as their witness. It was going to be a big surprise to the family, and they planned on making the announcement soon. Charlie and Kaitlin were going to sing the song they had written together for the occasion. Charlie informed his parents there was going to be a special celebration at the ranch Friday evening, and they were to attend.

"Is that a request or a statement?" Cathleen wanted to know.

"You wouldn't want to miss my duet with Kaitlin, now, would you?"

"Are you two singing her new song together?"

"It's a surprise, and if I told you, it wouldn't be one."

"You will have to see if your dad can get away early."

"Okay," said Charlie, "I will work on him."

Bridget didn't know how they had managed to keep their wedding a secret, and though she knew Cathleen was going to be upset about it, they did what they thought was best for the family. She had baked and decorated her own wedding cake, and they would all celebrate their union tonight at the ranch. Kaitlin's band was coming from Las Vegas, so it was sure to be spectacular. She and Charlie had been practicing their songs together, and Kaitlin would debut her new album. Aiden promised they would make it on time.

It was a beautiful afternoon with no rain in the forecast. There were colored lights everywhere, all around the entrance and in the area where the event would take place. A restaurant in the immediate area was catering the meal. Afterward, Bridget brought out her wedding cake. She and Kevin announced their wedding was in Las Vegas, and said they wanted to share the good news with the family. After Bridget showed off her ring, they cut the cake. Bridget smeared cake all over Kevin's face. He couldn't let her get away with that, so she got it right back! The music started as they wiped their faces. Kaitlin got up to sing her new single as cake and coffee were being served. Charlie stood up with her and announced that he and Kaitlin had written a song called "Together We Belong." Just for his parents, he dedicated it to his mom and dad and the newlyweds.

> *I saw you from across the room,*
> *A love we thought would never bloom.*
> *You smiled at me as you came my way.*
> *I wondered what I could say to make you stay.*
> *I went to take your hand as I said hello,*
> *But you said, "I really have to go."*
> *It took only one glance for me*
> *To want to get to know you.*
> *Together, together is where we belong.*
> *Now that you are here, it's forever, dear,*
> *For that's where the two of us belong.*
>
> *As we talked for hours on the steps that night,*
> *we both knew that this was right.*
> *It was like when we first met,*
> *The day I'll never forget.*
> *It was like magic when you spoke my name that day,*
> *And I'm so glad we felt the same way.*
> *With God all things are possible,*

And our lives He did entwine.
He has a purpose for everything,
And that's a very good sign!
Together, together is where we belong.
Now that you are here, it's forever, dear,
For that's where the two of us belong!

As Charlie and Kaitlin sang, Kevin and Bridget stood up and started dancing. Aiden reached for Cathleen's hand to join the newlyweds. She shook her head no, as she was afraid of stumbling, but Aiden whispered in her ear, "I won't let you fall, and if you start to, I'll be there to catch you." She just couldn't say no to that, so they joined Kevin and Bridget. Soon several couples were dancing. When the song was over, they got a standing ovation!

Cathleen found out that Kevin and Bridget had been staying in Cathleen's old apartment where she, Kaitlin, and Bridget had once lived. Now that everyone knew and the lease was almost up, they would look for a place of their own. Everyone was so happy for the newlyweds and asked why it had taken so long for Kevin to propose. Kevin said it wasn't him—he had just had to be a patient man until he wore Bridget down.

"She finally got tired of my nagging and said yes."

"So this is what you two have been up to," Cathleen said to Kaitlin and Charlie. "Well, you both sound very good. I wish only the best for you. Charlie, you definitely have been holding out on us. We knew Kaitlin was very talented, and we knew you were good, we just didn't know how good!"

Charleen couldn't hold it in any longer. "I knew about it, Mom, but I promised not to tell because Charlie told me not to."

They all laughed at her loyalty to her big brother and told her it was okay to keep a secret as long as it didn't hurt anyone. "Does this mean you have a new career?" his mom asked, "and aren't going to college?"

"No, ma'am, it just means I love to sing, and if something comes along for me in the music industry, I will check it out. Just as you knew what your passion in life was, I know what mine is. Whatever I decide to do with my life, I will never be too far away from you."

His mom said, "Don't stay out too late, you have a graduation coming up." Cathleen looked at Aiden and asked, "What do you think about what your son is doing?"

"Suits him, suits me," Aiden said. "You just never know what's in these Irish genes!"

When Cathleen and Aiden finally made it home, they were both exhausted. Aiden had already had a full day at the clinic and was nearly asleep before his head hit the pillow. Cathleen lay there letting everything soak in before finally drifting off to sleep. The dream had returned, but she couldn't make out who was in the field of flowers. It was like she was looking through a thick film and couldn't identify the people. When she awoke the next morning, she continued to be quite puzzled by the dream. What did it really mean, if anything, and why was it so different from her other dreams?

Chapter 37

Graduation day was Friday! Charlie was glad he had been able to attend the same high school as his mom and dad. They had a great basketball team, and he was their lead man. He set the record for the most baskets this year. He was also class valedictorian.

Aiden was proud of his son. Even though they shared the same love for basketball, they were not taking the same career paths. Charlie wasn't sure what he wanted to do, other than play basketball and sing. He didn't know if he wanted to go into the medical field but wasn't ruling anything out. Today was the last day he could pick up his cap and gown. Just one more shot and he would quit. He hurried to get dressed so he wouldn't miss the bus. His mom would meet him at the shop after Bridget picked her up at her office.

Once Charlie had picked up his cap and gown, he got a ride home with his friend Randy. Cathleen asked Bridget to take her by the food bank to see Maria, who had some information to give her. The investigator had been able to track down her half-sister's father, Jeremy Lancaster, and he was willing to talk to them. He said he had not contacted Deidre in years and had just recently found out about her and Darcy's death. He had been living in

New York all these years, and his daughter lived nearby. She was a designer for a well-known clothing firm and had never married. Maria said they would set up a time for them all to meet if everyone agreed—after Charlie's graduation, per Cathleen's request. She could tell Bridget was dying to know what was going on behind closed doors, but she would find out soon enough.

It wasn't long before Cathleen noticed the baby bump! Bridget hadn't told anyone yet but knew it was too obvious to keep hiding. Cathleen couldn't help but ask, "So when were you going to tell us?"

"I was going to tell you today when I saw you."

"So when is the new arrival expected?

"The doctor said we should have a Valentine baby, but we don't know the sex yet. We both want to know so we can be better prepared than you were with Charlie."

The family was happy about the upcoming event, for there had been no babies since Charleen. There had been such a turn of events when Kevin married Bridget. Now, instead of Bridget just being Cathleen's cousin, she was also her sister-in-law after marrying Kevin. It was funny trying to explain this to people

Charlie was hoping for a car for graduation, but he hadn't gotten any response from his hints. He felt they would come around to his way of thinking soon so he wouldn't have to keep borrowing his mom's car. Kaitlin was coming in tonight, and she and Charlie were going to perform at the ranch again. They were getting to be well known around town now, and some people just came out in the evenings now to eat and be entertained.

Kaitlin had been dating someone in her band, but that probably wouldn't last long. Charlie had been so busy; he had not had the time to get serious about anyone. He had dated Kelly, a girl in his class, and had taken her to the prom, but they weren't serious. He hadn't met anyone who could live up to his mom; maybe his expectations were too high, because she was one of a kind.

Charlie asked Kelly if she wanted to come hear him sing at the ranch tonight, and she said she would love to. She had never heard him sing before and was happy to be invited. She asked if she could bring her cousins, who were in town for the graduation, and Charlie said, "The more, the merrier!" What he didn't know was that they were from Nashville, Tennessee, which was considered the capital of country music. His dad couldn't make it, because he was seeing patients at the hospital tonight so he could be off for Charlie's graduation. Cathleen had said she would come and hear him another time.

Graduation went off without a hitch the next night. Some of the family members from Ireland came over for the graduation. Charlie gave a great speech, thanking his mom and dad for being the best parents a guy could have and for their guidance. When he received his diploma, Bridget and several family members stood up and yelled "Woohoo, Charlie, way to go," as Charlie's name was called. The schools tried to discourage outburst from the audience now, but his crazy family did it anyway.

They had the party at Bridget's Delicatessen and barely had room for everyone. Maria and her mom, Lupe, had pitched in, along with Kaitlin and Bridget's family. Outside the deli was a brand new Mustang with a big red bow on it. Charlie hadn't seen it until his dad handed him the keys. As Charlie hugged his dad, Aiden said, "Congratulations, son!" Charlie wanted to take the girls for a ride in it, but Aiden reminded him he had a party going on in his honor and could do that later.

Later that night, as they prepared for bed, Cathleen became restless. *Why can't I lie down and sleep like Aiden?* she wondered. He had always slept like a baby, while she tossed and turned before finally drifting off. She finally got up and retrieved her journal, which now lay on the table beside the bed. She wanted to remember the wonderful occasion, so went to the porch to write.

> *My precious Charlie,*
>
> *I still love saying your name, and I'm glad that we named you after your grandfather. He was a wonderful man, and I hope you follow in his footsteps. You graduated from high school with honors, making us so proud. You are considered a man now, although you will always be my little man. Dad and I are so very proud of the person you have become. Eighteen years ago, I wouldn't have thought this possible, but my faith was weak. Now I'm strong, and I know that if you follow God, He will take you wherever you desire, if it's in His will. I pray that you will keep the faith, and no matter what career you decide to follow, we will support you 100 percent.*
>
> *Always loving you!*
> *Mom*

Chapter 38

"How are you feeling?" Aunt Fiona asked Bridget.

"Well, we found out we're having a baby girl, so I am feeling very blessed, thank you. I am already starting to waddle like a duck."

"You will have to slow down soon and let Kevin take over some of your duties for a while," Fiona said. "He will make a good father, like his brother, and it's good to have a doctor and retired nurse in the family. Have you heard anything from Cathleen about Charlie? Has he made any decisions about college or what he wants to do now that he's graduated?"

"I think you should talk to Cathleen about that. She thinks I know too much of her business already, and I do, but I would rather it come from her."

Fiona was taking Cathleen for her checkup and would find out for herself. On the way, she asked about Charlie.

Cathleen said, "I haven't heard Charlie talking much about his future, but I did see him making eyes at one of Kelly's cousins. I saw that look from his dad when he was that age, so I am a little concerned."

"Who is Kelly?" Aunt Fiona asked.

"A girl he's been seeing who was in his class. He says he's not serious about her; she's just someone to hang out with. Her cousins came from Nashville to the graduation. The girl in question is Anna Marie, and she just graduated, too. She and Charlie seemed to hit it off. I don't think Kelly has a problem with it. They are both nice girls. Charlie has a good head on his shoulders, so I don't think there is anything to worry about."

The nurse called Cathleen into the doctor's office, and Fiona went in with her. The doctor said he had found out there was a new drug on the market, and even though it wasn't a sure cure, it had been found to ward off most of the symptoms Cathleen was having. It was also used for other illnesses as well. He didn't tell her it was an antidepressant because she would deny needing it. Being a nurse, Fiona was familiar with the drug, and encouraged her to try it.

"I've spoken to Aiden about this already," the doctor said, "and he said if it was okay with you, it wouldn't hurt to try it."

"When can I start?"

"I'll call you in a prescription today," he said.

Cathleen was reeling with the good news; just the thought of the new medication made her feel better. They decided to go by the deli and have lunch at Bridget's.

"Now that you know you're having a girl, have you thought about names yet?" Cathleen asked Bridget.

"Yes, but there's so many to choose from, and we want to pick one we both like. So far, we haven't agreed on one." Cathleen shared the good news with her sister-in-law about the new drug, and they had everyone toasting good luck to them both before they left.

Bridget was using the same ob-gyn doctor Cathleen had used. The following week, Bridget asked her if she would go with her for her checkup while Kevin ran the deli. Bridget told Cathleen they had finally agreed on a name for the baby: Brianna Kerry O'Leary. Kevin let her have her way anyway—she had to carry the load, after all.

Bridget's pregnancy brought the two women even closer than before. They still bickered, but that was what made their relationship so unique. It was all in fun, and after all was said and done, they were still friends. They shopped together, argued over who had bought the cutest clothes and who had the cutest husband, and then would go back to the deli for lunch. Cathleen always used her walker wherever she went. She hoped the medicine would change all that, but she couldn't afford to take any chances with her health. Bridget was in no condition to help her. She had gained twenty pounds already and had several months to go.

A group of the ladies had started getting together at the church on Thursdays and making baby blankets. They had made one for Charleen when she was born, and now they were making one for Bridget's baby. The rest were to be given out to the families in need that Cathleen and Maria worked with.

Maria had become such a good friend and handled a lot of Cathleen's affairs. She was glad to see Maria and Geoffrey were getting along so well. He adored her and had been trying to get her to marry him, but she wasn't ready to settle down yet. She would do it in her own time, and knew Geoffrey wasn't going anywhere.

Chapter 39

C harlie came in from playing ball. After his shower, he went into the kitchen to talk to his mom. She was teaching Charleen how to cook the Irish stew from the recipe Aunt Fiona had given her.

"What's up Charlie?"

"Well, I've been thinking—I have gotten a couple of scholarship offers and could play basketball if I wanted to, but I've been thinking about trying to get my feet wet in the music industry first. Kelly's cousins' family knows a lot of people in Nashville, and they think if I visited the city and distributed Kaitlin's and my record, we may have a chance of recording it. I can still come back and go to college."

"Is this what you want to do or what Kaitlin thinks you should do?" Cathleen asked.

"We're in agreement that this could be a good thing for us both and could open new doors for both of us. I don't plan on being gone long, and Kaitlin still has her gig in Vegas to go back to if things don't work out for her. I can always go to college."

"You know I would never stop you from doing what you love. I don't think your dad would, either, but you will be back in a few months, won't you?"

"Yes, ma'am, I will," Charlie said. "Thanks for being so understanding. I'll talk to Dad later. I have to run now. I'm meeting Anna Marie for lunch, and then I'm taking her out to the ranch."

"Have fun, and don't drive like your aunt Bridget!" Cathleen called after him.

Cathleen had planned to meet with Maria to see how things had gone with the investigator and her half-sister's father, so she decided to volunteer at the food bank and check in at her office. Maria told her she had spoken to Cathleen's newfound sister, Victoria, and her dad, Jeremy, and they agreed that it was time for the sisters to meet. Cathleen was eager to meet Victoria and find out more about her. Victoria's dad had already told her all about her mother, Darcy. The three women decided to meet at Bridget's deli that afternoon.

Maria and Cathleen arrived before Victoria. As they watched for her at a table by the window, Cathleen told Maria that Victoria would be wearing a butterfly pin on her suit so they couldn't mistake her. Cathleen hadn't told Bridget anything yet, but Bridget could tell something was up and was waiting for Cathleen to tell her.

The door opened, and a lovely, dark-haired beauty walked in with a beautiful butterfly pin on her jacket. Cathleen would never have recognized her sister if she hadn't known about the butterfly. She had such grace about her—a grace Cathleen had once had. Maria called out to her as she approached their table and asked, "Are you Victoria?"

"Yes," the woman replied. Maria introduced herself and shook her hand.

"And you must be Cathleen," Victoria said. "We have so much to catch up on, but I'm starving for some good Irish food. Can we order now?"

"Of course," Cathleen said, laughing as she motioned for Bridget to come take their order. Bridget waddled over to their table, and Cathleen introduced her as the owner of the deli but didn't tell her who Victoria was. Bridget gave Cathleen a funny look, but nothing else was said.

While they were waiting for their food, Victoria explained that her dad had a business meeting he couldn't get out of but would love to meet with them another time. As they talked, Cathleen noticed that Victoria's eyes were the color of their mother's and that she had the same sweet smile. Victoria told them a little about her job but wanted to know more about her new family. They agreed to get together again when they could.

"And now that we're family, please call me Vicky."

Cathleen was glad she would finally be able to tell her family. Bridget caught up with Cathleen as she and Maria were leaving and asked, "Is there a secret here, or can anyone know what's going on?" She had tried to eavesdrop but found it too hard to get close enough without looking obvious.

"I'll let you know when the time is right," remarked Cathleen. She loved knowing something that Bridget didn't know first. *What she doesn't know won't hurt her,* Cathleen thought as she left the deli. Maria took her to the food bank, and one of the delivery guys dropped her off at Aiden's office later, where she waited for him to get off work so they could ride home together. He never turned patients down, and sometimes he was late getting away. Today was one of those days. Cathleen had picked up dinner from Bridget's deli, so there would be no kitchen duty tonight. She hadn't been sure how the meeting would go with Vicky, so she hadn't said anything to Aiden yet.

Chapter 40

Cathleen had finally started feeling better on the new drug. However, she still seemed worried about Charlie and Charleen, and she talked to Aiden about it on the way home from the office. Aiden reminded her how young she had been when she lost her parents, and her mothers hadn't died from the disease. She had to have faith that Charlie and Charleen carried the same gene of responsibility she had at their age. She had to believe that Charlie and Charleen would be fine. He reminded her of the progress being made in the medical field and how well she was doing now. He could tell that the older she got, the more she worried about her family.

Then he changed the subject and talked about how some of her patients he treated were doing. Thank goodness they had caught most of the abusers in one family; some had gone to jail, and others were in counseling. The little girl who'd had so many broken bones had been treated for osteoporosis and was growing into a lovely young woman with no ill effects from the disease. She wanted to tell him about meeting her half-sister but still didn't feel it was the right time. She knew she had to tell the family soon.

Living outside the city had its drawbacks. Charleen was going to a new school now, but had adjusted well, and Cathleen had more freedom to get outside. The new drug made her feel so much better, and she felt like getting out more. It was a longer commute to the city, but she didn't mind. The good thing was she was closer to the horse ranch. She loved living on one level now and not having to use elevators. She had a wonderful view from her front porch of red maple trees and a lovely array of flowers she loved. She would sit for hours watching the birds and the bees swarming around the flowers. She even caught occasional glimpses of butterflies and was reminded of how her mom loved watching them. Now she seemed to be repeating the past.

She loved to go with Charleen to the park nearby after school and on weekends to enjoy nature with her daughter, something she had never been able to do with the mother who had raised her. Cathleen was grateful she had lived longer than her mothers had and was still able to function on her own. She could sit on her porch and enjoy the view of God's creation whenever she chose, and her outlook on life seemed to be better now on the new drug.

She was still having trouble sleeping, and tonight was one of those nights. She got up and as she went to the porch to write in her journal, she noticed the picture on the wall. Several months ago, Charleen had asked her mother to sit for her so she could paint a portrait of her, and Cathleen had forgotten about it. She had not seen the painting before, so Charleen must have put it up recently, after having it framed. As Cathleen gazed at the painting, she saw the picture of her mother Darcy painted in the background. How that girl had captured this image was unbelievable. Charleen had never seen her grandmother, as far as Cathleen knew. She would have to ask her daughter how this had happened.

Cathleen stirred when she heard Charlie coming in. He called her name, and she said, "I'm awake, son. What time is it?"

"After 1:00 a.m.," he said. "I had to drop off Kelly and her cousins. How long have you been out here?"

"Too long, I'm afraid. I'm surprised your dad hasn't come looking for me. I've been sitting out here for a while now and must have drifted off."

"Well, let's get you back to bed before he knows you're gone," Charlie said, locking up as they went in.

Chapter 41

Winter had finally set in, with snow everywhere, and the holidays had come and gone. Not many people were visiting the horse ranch now, so things were slow, though Bridget kept busy at her delicatessen and bakery, and Dr. O'Leary still had to tend to his sick babies. Yes, everyone had to eat, and babies got sick, so business was still good for the O'Leary families. Cathleen had been talking to Vicky, and they were making plans to meet at the ranch when the weather warmed up and everyone could be there.

Bridget's baby was due anytime, so everyone was anxiously waiting for the phone call. Kerry was going to fly on over from Ireland so she would be here in time. It was now February, and the doctor said it could be any day now, and everyone was guessing what the birthdate might be. Cathleen still thought it would be a Valentine baby, because sometimes babies are late for first-time mothers.

Kevin went to pick up his mother-in-law from the airport and discovered his mom, Abigail, had come, too. She said she didn't want to miss this special event either and that her husband could handle the business without her for a while. Besides, she needed a vacation. The condo Kevin and Bridget lived in was quite crowded with four adults. There were three bedrooms, but one of them had been made into a nursery, which meant the two women would have to share a bed and bathroom. They had offered to stay at a hotel near the hospital, but the family would have none of that. Bridget said it was time they got to know each other better anyway!

Aiden took the call early on February 2, Groundhog Day— Brianna Kerry couldn't wait until the fourteenth. Thank goodness it was morning, so everyone could make arrangements to meet in the maternity waiting room.

It was a difficult first birth for Bridget, and they could hear her yelling all the way down the hall. Finally, after five hours, the doctor gave her something to ease her pain, and she still ended up having a cesarean section performed. After the baby went to the nursery, they all went to the window to see what had caused Bridget so much pain. Baby Brianna lay there, a curly-headed bundle of joy sucking her thumb without a care in the world. The groundhog had not seen his shadow, so maybe it would start warming up soon. Meanwhile, Bridget was asking for more pain medicine and telling Kevin this was his one and only child from her. She could not go through this again! Mothers had been back several more times after those words had been spoken. The nurses just smiled when they heard it.

Mother and child got to go home three days later. Brianna had two grandmothers doting on her, so Bridget milked it for all it was worth. She knew they would be gone soon, so she let them play nanny while she rested from her surgery. She still had a business to run, so she needed to get well quickly. Two weeks later, Abigail and Kerry flew back to Ireland. Bridget sure hated to see them go.

Cathleen had her own family and health to attend to. Kaitlin had gone back to Las Vegas.

"Well, it's just you and me now, kid," Bridget said to Brianna while nursing her. She read it was better to breast-feed if you could, and Bridget wanted a healthy, smart baby like her parents had had. Cathleen called her daily to check on her. She found out the best time to call her was around 6:00 p.m., when Bridget wasn't asleep; otherwise, she got a cranky person on the line!

Chapter 42

Charlie and Kaitlin had flown to Nashville to meet with some of Anna Marie's friends in the music industry. He still wasn't sure what he wanted but felt it couldn't hurt. Kelly's cousins had lived there all their lives, so they knew practically everyone. If they didn't know someone, they knew someone who did. Kaitlin said Charlie could share her apartment.

Charlie had never thought of himself as a country singer, but he spent a lot of time rehearsing country songs. He had the ability to sing anything and the drive to make it work, but he loved country, so he started writing country lyrics and putting them to music. Now he just had to find someone who believed he could pull it off. Kaitlin, meanwhile, was working on another new recording.

Anna Marie's dad was friends with a man who worked for a well-known record company, so she talked him into getting Charlie an audition. Her dad had never heard Charlie sing, but he was willing to ask for a favor for his baby girl. Charlie would either sink or swim. The man would make his daughter happy either way.

Charlie walked over to the studio next morning with his guitar and sweaty palms. He couldn't remember when he had been this nervous. He went in and introduced himself, and the man in the control room showed him where he needed to go and said to let him know when he was ready. Charlie handed him a copy of the sheet music and took his position. When it was over, the man shook his hand and thanked him for coming.

That's it? Charlie thought as he walked back to his apartment, not really knowing what they thought of his singing or his song. Not even Anna Marie heard anything for about a week; then her dad called Charlie and said they would like to get his permission to play it on air and get the public's opinion on whether to trash it or treasure it. It turned out to be an overwhelming treasure, and Charlie was to get his first big break. He was happy about it, but he missed his family.

Charlie went back home and was thinking about enrolling in one of the scholarship universities when he got a call from Nashville wanting him to sign a record deal. He hated to leave his mom so soon, so he sat down and talked to her about it.

"Remember what I told you, Charlie, when we discussed this before? I told you I would support you in whatever direction you chose to go, and Dad said the same. You must go where your heart tells you. If it doesn't work out for you, you are still young enough to still go to college and pursue another career," Cathleen said. "But before you leave, I have someone I want you and Charleen to meet. Your dad is coming home early, and I want you and Charleen to meet us at the ranch tonight. Be prepared to sing your new song for us."

"You're the best mom and dad a guy could ever have," he said as he picked up his phone to make reservations to fly back to Nashville.

When Vicky came to the ranch with Cathleen, everyone was wondering who she was—everyone that is but Aiden. Cathleen learned that Aiden had actually met Vicky when he was going to school in California. She was living there at the time and dating one of the interns. Aiden and Vicky knew many of the same people here in New York and had run into each other from time to time. He just didn't know the two were related.

She seemed to fit right in with the family. It was a big but welcome surprise to know there was another family member living in New York!

Charleen was in high school now, and it was still hard for Cathleen to believe her children were growing up and making their own decisions now. She knew better than to try to talk Charlie out of what he loved doing. He got his stubbornness from her and his dad. And she was in awe of Charleen and her contentment while sitting and painting. She loved to sing as well. Cathleen would hear her humming as she sat and painted outside. She didn't know where Charleen's imagination as an artist came from, but it was extraordinary. According to Vicky's dad, Jeremy, Darcy had loved to draw when they were married, so maybe it was in the family after all. Cathleen thought of the things she had heard about "starving artists" and hoped Charleen could move on to something more lucrative as she got older, but that was her daughter's decision to make. Maybe there was still hope for her to go into the medical field.

Later that week, when Charleen came home from school, Cathleen was sitting on the porch, looking at the picture Charleen had painted of her. Her daughter put her books up and came out with a glass of lemonade for each of them. She thought this was the perfect time to ask her daughter how she had come to paint the picture of her with a woman she had never seen.

"But I have, Mom. Remember when I was a little girl, and I went into the hospital to have my heart fixed?"

"Yes, I remember it very well."

"Well, you weren't there, but an angel was, and she held my hand and comforted me. This is how I remember her."

"So you knew who she was?"

"Yes, ma'am" Charleen said.

"Oh" was all Cathleen could say. It was odd that Charleen had seen her grandmother as an angel, but she was only three then and thought as a three year old. She had seen pictures of angels but had never seen her grandmother, as far as Cathleen knew.

"Also, I've been thinking I may want to go to nursing school. Aunt Fiona and Dad are both so good at what they do, and I think I would be too. Painting is fun, but I need a career, and I'm not sure I want to paint for a living. But I will sell my work if anyone is interested. Besides, I don't graduate for three more years. Charlie has left town, and I don't want to go too far away from you and Dad. You still need me."

Cathleen's eyes misted over with tears. "That is the sweetest thing you could have said to me, sweetheart, and I know Daddy will be glad to hear you have some of his genes. But don't do it for me or him. Do it for yourself. Then you will never regret your decision."

Chapter 43

Three years later

As the years passed, Cathleen was holding her own on her medicine, and her life had taken on a new meaning. Charleen loved helping her mom out doing chores around the house, just as Cathleen had loved helping her mom. Cathleen had taught Charleen to cook when she was younger, and Charleen had become quite the cook and baker.

Charlie would call every week and said he loved it there in Nashville, but he said he would be making a trip back soon. He wouldn't miss his little sister's approaching graduation for anything.

Cathleen had managed to outlive both of her moms so far and had two wonderful children and a husband she adored. Vicky fit right in with the family when they could get together. When Charleen found out that Vicky worked for a design firm, she wanted to know all about how she had gotten started in the business. Cathleen was afraid Charleen would be a nuisance to her, but Vicky assured her she wasn't and loved being a part of her life.

Bridget's daughter, Brianna, was three now and a handful, just like her mother had been. Bridget would bring her out to Cathleen's when she could, and they would go over to the horse ranch for a little while. Cathleen had not been back on a horse since her accident but was content to guide the younger children around the ranch.

Cathleen's front porch was still her favorite place to be. She loved sitting there in the peaceful surroundings she now called home. Charleen would be graduating soon. Cathleen was so proud of her children's accomplishments. What mattered most to her was that they were happy and healthy. Charlie would be coming home in two weeks for the graduation, and he mentioned Anna Marie might be coming with him.

Charleen had chosen to go to nursing school in New York, so she would be close to her parents. She was really a daddy's girl, but her mom needed her the most. She had sold some of her paintings but had not told her parents yet. She wanted to surprise them after graduation. She had chosen not to pursue her love of art. She felt she was as good as she needed to be at this time in her life. She wanted to concentrate on taking care of others now. She would learn all that in nursing school. Apparently, she did have some of both of her families' genes.

Charlie called home and spoke to Charleen. He said he would be home next week in time for the graduation and a quick visit before heading back to Nashville. Charleen told him Mom seemed down in the dumps lately and that her headaches had returned, but she said she didn't know if it was from stress or because she was graduating. Charlie then made the decision to come alone. He intended to stay home longer than planned. He wanted to make sure his mom was okay before leaving again.

Cathleen had not been feeling well lately and wondered if the headaches and sleeplessness were side effects from her medication. Her daughter was graduating, and now her babies were practically grown. *Isn't that what I've prayed for?* she thought. She had managed to survive by God's grace and her own sheer will and determination, and she felt her prayers had been heard. She was looking forward to her baby girl graduating, and nothing but death was going to stop her from being there.

What she didn't know was that Charlie would be coming through the door that evening. He had called Charleen to pick him up at the airport in his Mustang. He had never let her drive it before, so she was more than happy to. He told her not to tell Mom, because he wanted to surprise her. He was glad he had made the decision to leave his car at his parents' so he could come and go whenever he wanted. Everyone was home when they pulled up— even Aunt Fiona had dropped by—and wanted to know all about his new music career and whether he would continue to sing. He said he still wasn't sure about anything right now and didn't want to make any decisions yet.

"I'm here to be with my family for now, and that's all I want to concentrate on," he said. "And just look at my little sister—all grown up and graduating. Mom, you don't have babies anymore."

"You'll always be my babies. Both of you."

Cathleen was determined to be at Charleen's graduation, and with the help of Fiona and her medication, she had managed to be ready in time. Vicky was coming, and Kevin and Bridget would be there with Brianna. Kaitlin had flown in the day before. It turned out to be a beautiful day, so the ceremony was outdoors this time around. As Charleen walked up to get her diploma, Vicky, Kevin, Bridget, and Kaitlin stood up and yelled, "Woohoo! Way to go, Charleen!" Charleen had expected this to happen and just laughed at her crazy relatives!

Chapter 44

Now that Charleen had graduated and Charlie was sticking around to visit everyone, things were getting back to normal. While she still could, Cathleen wanted to write in her journal, so she brought it with her to the front porch and got comfortable in her lounge chair. She didn't realize how tired she was until she started to write.

My dearest Charlie and Charleen,

How so very proud I am of you and your accomplishments. You each set out on a different path, but I realize it's not the path that matters so much as the goal you set before you, and you both seem to be achieving your own. All your father and I want is for you to be happy. We couldn't ask for more than that. I just had to tell you one more time while I could still write and tell you how very much I love you and how proud I am of you!

Always loving you both,
Mom

She put the pen down as sleep overcame her.

Charlie and Charleen came in together and found their mom slumped over in the lounge chair, eyes closed, with the journal in her lap. "Mom, are you okay?" they both asked, fearful of what they were seeing.

Cathleen opened her eyes and said, "Yes, I'm fine. I just had the most serene dream. It was about Grandfather Charlie. He looked younger than I remembered, but I knew it was him. He was walking down a hill toward me into this beautiful field of flowers with my cocker spaniel, Daisy, and he was singing an Irish lullaby, letting me know that everything was going to be okay. He told me he would see me soon. It was like he was reassuring me." Cathleen's voice seemed to grow stronger as she told her kids of the dream.

"Well, let's go in and celebrate," said Charlie, locking up and helping his mom into the house.

She was beginning to realize she was having more frequent headaches. She hadn't been concerned about them at first, but now they seemed more intense. Aiden noticed her bottle of pain pills on the bedside table and asked her about it. She admitted she had been taking more of them than usual because of the pain.

"We need to make an appointment with Dr. Li if you're having this much pain."

"I think its stress because of everything going on lately with graduation and Charlie coming home. I'll be fine in a few days."

"Well, you're going anyway. Dr. Li can determine how fine you are."

"Oh, Aiden, I just need to rest more," she said, closing her eyes and drifting off to sleep.

Cathleen wanted more than anything for everything to be okay, but her body didn't lie. She knew it well enough to know she wasn't doing well, but she was still a fighter. Charlie was still in town, and he and Charleen had been spending a lot of time at the ranch with the kids. It made her happy to know they were following her dream. She knew Charlie would be going back to Nashville soon and Charleen would be going to nursing school.

One afternoon, Fiona visited and noticed Cathleen seemed more tired than usual. As she was getting ready to leave, Fiona asked her, "Are you sure you are okay until Aiden gets home?"

"Yes, I'm fine. Let me get my journal, and I'll sit on the porch for a while."

They hugged, and Cathleen said, "Thank you so much for all you have done for me and my family. I don't know what we would have done without you!"

"Oh, you would have found a way, but it wouldn't have been anywhere near as much fun!"

They both laughed. "I Love you," they said in unison. Cathleen sat there for a while just looking at the beautiful landscape, thinking of all the work that had gone in to making this home so beautiful and accessible for her. She picked up her pen and began to write.

Chapter 45

Aiden found her with her journal still open in her hand. She was wearing her favorite floral caftan that he had given her for her birthday and she had the most peaceful look on her face. He felt for a pulse, but there was none. He brushed her hair back and kissed her for the last time. Her right hand was clutching her wedding ring, the claddagh ring that her grandfather had given her many years ago. Her body was still warm to the touch as he cradled her in his arms, knowing she was gone.

"Remember the promise I made you many years ago—that I would always take care of you and love you no matter what?" he asked her. "Well, I'm still here, and I love you more than I ever thought possible."

He placed her gently back on the lounge chair as he dried his eyes. He called the coroner's office first, because it would take them awhile to get here. Then he called Charlie. He told him to tell his sister that the angels had come to take their mother home. They did an autopsy, and the coroner said she had had an aneurysm.

Family and friends attended her burial on top of the hill overlooking the front porch. Beside her grave was a beautiful red maple tree, and the flowers she had so loved were nestled on the hill above. There were black-eyed susans, begonias, lavender, irises and daisies. Charleen painted a beautiful cross with some of her mom's favorite flowers on it and wrote her mom's favorite Scripture: "With God, all things are possible" (Matthew 19:26). Aiden brought her journal to the cemetery and read the last page she wrote.

My dearest family,

I just have to let you know while I still can that you have been my dream come true, and I couldn't have asked for a better husband or children. I am so thankful God has let me live long enough see all of your accomplishments. I have had a wonderful life.

Aiden, thank you for giving me what I most desired in life: a loving husband and two wonderful children!

Charlie and Charleen, you are gifts from God, and you have both made me so happy. What a blessing you have been to Dad and me.

Vicky, how happy I am to have a sister like you. You have truly been an awesome addition to our family.

Grandfather Charlie's last wish was for us to all come to know the Lord, and I'm so glad we have done that.

Always loving you all.

They each went up and placed flowers on her grave. Out of nowhere, the most beautiful monarch butterflies came and landed on the flowers. The members of her family each held a balloon. When they released them, they spelled out, "We'll see you soon."

What more could an Irish girl want?!

Printed in the United States
By Bookmasters